EDITORS
Susan Burmeister-Brown
Linda Burmeister Davies

CONSULTING EDITORS
Annie Callan
Dave Chipps
Britney Gress
Tamara Moan

COPY EDITOR & PROOFREADER
Scott Allie

TYPESETTING & LAYOUT
Heidi Weitz Siegel

COVER ILLUSTRATOR
Jane Zwinger

STORY ILLUSTRATOR
Jon Leon

PUBLISHED QUARTERLY
in spring, summer, fall, and winter by
Glimmer Train Press, Inc.
710 SW Madison Street, Suite 504
Portland, Oregon 97205-2900 U.S.A.
Telephone: 503/221-0836
Facsimile: 503/221-0837

PRINTED IN U.S.A.

Glimmer Train (ISSN #1055-7520), registered in U.S. Patent and Trademark Office, is published quarterly, $29 per year in the U.S., by Glimmer Train Press, Inc., Suite 504, 710 SW Madison, Portland, OR 97205. Second-class postage paid at Portland, OR, and additional mailing offices. POSTMASTER: Send address changes to Glimmer Train Press, Inc., Suite 504, 710 SW Madison, Portland, OR 97205.

ISSN # 1055-7520, ISBN # 1-880966-21-2, CPDA BIPAD # 79021

DISTRIBUTION: Bookstores can purchase *Glimmer Train Stories* through these distributors:
Anderson News Co., 6016 Brookvale Ln., #151, Knoxville, TN 37919
Bernhard DeBoer, Inc., 113 E. Centre St., Nutley, NJ 07110
Ingram Periodicals, 1226 Heil Quaker Blvd., LaVergne, TN 37086
IPD, 674 Via de la Valle, #204, Solana Beach, CA 92075
Peribo PTY Ltd., 58 Beaumont Rd., Mt. Kuring-Gai, NSW 2080, AUSTRALIA
Ubiquity, 607 Degraw St., Brooklyn, NY 11217

SUBSCRIPTION SVCS: EBSCO, Faxon, READMORE

Subscription rates: One year, $29 within the U.S. (Visa/MC/check).
Airmail to Canada, $39; outside North America, $49.
Payable by Visa/MC or check for U.S. dollars drawn on a U.S. bank.

Attention short-story writers: We pay $500 for first publication and onetime anthology rights. Please include a self-addressed, sufficiently stamped envelope with your submission. **Send manuscripts in January, April, July, and October.** *Send a SASE for guidelines, which will include information on our Short-Story Award for New Writers.*

Dedication

We dedicate this issue to
the solid voice of Eudora Welty.

Like a vain dream, Sara began to have thoughts of
spring and summer. At first she thought only simply, of
the colors of green and red, the smell of the sun on the
ground, the touch of leaves and of warm ripening
tomatoes. Then, all hidden as she was under the quilt,
she began to imagine and remember the town of
Dexter in the shipping season. There, in her mind,
dusty little Dexter became the theater for almost
legendary festivity, a place of pleasure. On every road
leading in, smiling farmers were bringing in wagon-
loads of the most beautiful tomatoes. The packing
sheds at Dexter Station were all decorated—no, it
was simply that the May sun was shining.
—*from "The Whistle" by Eudora Welty*

At last! Spring!

Susan & Linde

ONTENTS

ONTENTS

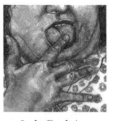

Mary Overton

My parents both have perfect copybook handwriting, so I don't know which one wrote on the back, "Mary's Santa Claus Hat, Christmas, 1955." I am posing in front of our Jetburgh, Missouri rented house, conveniently near the two-room school where my mom taught twenty-five first and second graders, while my dad served as principal and managed forty students in grades three through six. Mom was twenty-two. Dad was twenty-four. The Eureka school district paid them $2,200 and $3,300 respectively.

La Questa Press is publishing Mary Overton's first book in September. It's a collection of short fiction, half of which has appeared in various small literary magazines. Twelve years ago, Overton chose the title of her short story, "The Wine of Astonishment," for the book she hoped one day to publish. Another small press is now scheduled to reprint a novel with that same name, so she is looking for a new title.

Overton lives in Fairfax County, Virginia, with her husband and daughter. She teaches fourth grade.

Mary Overton [signature]

MARY OVERTON

Letters to Ellen

2/23/71

Dear Ellen,

Of course I will save your letters, but you must agree to keep mine. That way our biographers can work together. They will be a husband-wife team and they will divorce over us. They will quarrel about our significance and become intellectual enemies and wage a custody battle over our papers. Do you want to be responsible for the ruin of their lives? Quick. Destroy my letters. All two of them.

I know in the same time you have sent me fourteen letters. You remind me of it each time you write. That I can count them is proof I have saved them. My Intro Psych class explains this— the letters, not the counting. We are both anal, but I am the constipated sort, nurturing my hard little nuggets of shit, reluctant to let them go, and you are of the diarrheic personality, spewing your crap through a fire hose. Actually, I made that up. I haven't been to Psych class in two weeks. I haven't been to any class in two weeks. It hurts too much to get out of bed. I think my nerve endings have been damaged, burnt away by a sinister gas pumped into our dorm. Lots of girls don't get up in the mornings. February just is not worth living through. I went to the clinic and they gave me yellow pills that make my mouth dry and puffy. Why would a dry, puffy mouth help me through February and Intro Psych? I went to the fellow who teaches my section of Art History, and she said my concerns are common, blah, blah, blah. She said I sound like an indecisive grad student. That made me feel better. I've always wanted the afflictions of my elders. The problems of my own age are mundane.

I smoke now. I had to learn so I can smoke grass. You will not approve. Neither does my roommate. I have to go next door. There's a rich girl (her father is vice president of some evil capitalistic corporation) who has a single room that is an absolute pigsty. She must be desperate for friends because her room is available for anything. I go there and smoke and listen to the stereo. I do it as much to escape my roommate who doesn't talk to me anymore. My roommate's a country girl with a boyfriend who wears overalls. She drinks beer like a Viking. She's the only girl on our floor with her own car, which makes it bad that we don't get along, but we don't and I'm not sure why. I wrote a paper for her on Malcolm X and it got a B-minus. She's gotten locked out of the dorm five times (curfew is 11:30) and I've let her in the back door. Once I let in her hayseed boyfriend and gave them the room while I slept with the rich girl. I've gone home with both of them, the country girl and the rich girl, and each time I got so drunk I threw up. But I sent thank-you notes. Both sets of parents said they'd never gotten thank-you notes from a college kid.

Two weeks ago Tuesday I missed curfew, and I needed to pull an all-nighter for a paper due Wednesday. My roommate wouldn't let me in and I couldn't wake the rich girl, no matter how much I banged on her window. I'd spent the evening at a group house off campus that's not university students but drifters and hitchhikers and cosmic white-lightning people. They've got aluminum wrap sealed over the windows. The ceiling is draped with Indian bedspreads. The freezer has more acid than ice cubes. Anybody can sleep there and does, but I felt safer walking the streets all night. It was clear and cold so I had to walk fast. My face got numb but the rest of me burned like a furnace. The small-town streets here are wide and dark and empty. There are more stars here than at home. Orion has drifts of stars like veils across him. I felt like I could become my own myth and fall into the sky beside him and become a new constellation.

At six the library opened. I charged in to do my paper. How I thought I would write it without a pencil or a note card I don't know, but I was filled with elation. I pulled out books only to find that in each one, my pages were cut out with a razor blade. How odd, I thought, that someone destructive would share my topic. I looked in other books and found the same thing. Every one had been mutilated. I opened tens of books and then hundreds of books, leaving them like droppings behind me, making a trail of unsteady piles on the floor as I weaved through the silent, early-morning stacks. The books had no endings. From each one had been cut random pages, but always the conclusion and the index and the appendices. I returned to my room and went to bed and mostly have stayed there. The pills make me sleepy enough to ignore my roommate. I will not end this by asking you to write because you always do.

With love,

Mona

P.S. I don't believe you. How can you read *War and Peace* in one night?

4/6/73

Dear Ellen,

How unutterably contented I am, cow-like in the extreme, in a blissful, cow-like way. I feel sorry for anyone in the world who is not pregnant. Perhaps carrying a baby is like spring, sweeter than other seasons because its days are numbered and so brief.

Congratulations on your scholarship. Ten years from now you

will be a professor at Bard. You will be published in all the right journals, renowned for your slightly eccentric but level-headed ways, for your astounding insights all the more breathtaking because they come from a small, modest woman in sensible walking shoes. Am I correct? I have not seen you in two years. Tell me you have not changed. Lifetimes have passed since our last summer together. Civilizations have risen and fallen. Your mother has walked that drooling mutt of yours 1,460 times, a true test of maternal devotion.

Your letters are collecting in our post-office box. Please keep sending them. They will be all the more delightful, read at one time, in order, whenever we return to Redlands. Right now we are in Arizona, but we have no address. We live in the school bus. Sean and Randy spent the last month working in the copper mine because the engine blew up. Rita and I make hats that we sell sometimes to little stores and sometimes off a card table beside the road. You have never seen such hats, like opium dreams, full of feathers and rhinestones and nylon-net veils. I make my own tortillas, patting them hand to hand in a cloud of flour. An old Mexican woman showed me how. We used to be strict vegetarians, all four of us plus Rita's baby, but I learned as we became poor that such habits belong to the bourgeoisie. Dumpster diving is a sport I had to quit because of being pregnant. I have the nose of a bloodhound. I cannot stand the smells. I do double duty as guard and baby-sitter, and when Randy finds an unopened can of corned-beef hash then we happily put it in the rice and beans.

Last week I went to the free clinic for a check of the baby. Sometimes I feel like a Tupperware container with this lively little fish sealed inside of me. She talks to me. I haven't told Randy because he's getting into weird religious stuff with some Mexicans he met in the mines. If he knew I really talk with the baby he'd want me to go see their priest or guru or shaman or whatever they call this nasty old man who leads ceremonies out in the desert. I think they kill chickens and dance.

The baby talks to me conversationally. It's the way we live, I imagine, that lets me hear her. We don't have a lot of modern noise in our lives, not even toilets flushing. Think about how often toilets flush in a house where lots of people live. It's noise. The bus broke down on this road in the desert about two miles outside town. We put up awnings on the north side because the bus gets too hot in the day. We play rummy at night, or we make music. Until recently, and I'll tell you the story, I still had the flute I played in high school. Do you remember how we met, third-period band, Mrs. Kneebler, silent K? I used to watch you all puffed up and turning red over your oboe and wonder how anybody could pick such an embarrassing instrument. I don't know an A-sharp from a treble clef anymore, but I like to play in the desert at night, just these made-up things that might be background music for *Alice in Wonderland*. Sean plays guitar and writes songs about the meaninglessness of suburbia. Rita plays harmonica and Jew's harp. Randy is into rhythm. He beats on things. I wish we played every night, but it's hard to get the others to start unless we have a visitor and the guys want to show off how cool they are.

It's so quiet at night under the desert moon, I hear the bubbles when the baby turns inside me. Her name is Nirvana, and she tells me not to seek happiness, that all I long for I already am, I already have. I hold my big happy stomach and her voice links me to the uncountable, faceless, forgotten women with whom I share this sacrifice of my body. I tell Nirvana that, yes, I am at peace, but I cannot stop longing for a daily bath.

I went to the free clinic where the waiting room is wall-to-wall bellies, mostly Mexican girls and traveling hippie girls. The volunteers are good-hearted, middle-aged ladies, League-of-Women-Voters-type ladies, their children mostly grown and off being successful, the ladies wanting to adopt us all, the way you want to take home the puppies in pet-store windows. I found my benefactress filing gray folders in endless metal file drawers. She was so earnest about it. I heard her singing the alphabet song under her breath. I told her about you and your mother, only I said you were my family, and I told her about how Randy could fix anything, even the bus engine he was rebuilding. I told her how the baby Nirvana talked to me, only I said it was in dreams. She took me home for lunch and she let me have a long soak in her tub while she washed my clothes. Then she drove me out to the edge of town and I said I better walk the rest of the way so Rita didn't get jealous. The lady said, Okay, she had to hurry anyway to beat her husband home because he didn't like it when she brought down-and-out strangers to the house. He said she was going to get hurt someday doing it.

When I got to the bus it was vacant and abandoned looking, like some deserted refugee camp. After the coolness, the orderliness of the lady's house, our place seemed sinister. "She's gone," Nirvana said, clear as glass. "Rita's gone and taken her baby." Nirvana was right, of course. Rita left a note about how she'd gotten her dad to wire her money and for Sean not to go looking for her because by the time he got this message she and little Celestial would be on a Greyhound bus for home. She took all the secret hat-making money we were hiding from the guys, and she took some of the baby clothes I'd been collecting from churches and shelters. That was okay. But, Ellen, she took my flute. It was our last tangible connection, you and me. I am stripped bare of every proof of you. It's this life we lead, possessionless and homeless. I have molted so many times in the past two years that I have, without planning it, lost the souvenirs of my youth. Please send a photo of the two of us. Your mother took scads of them. I will make a shrine for it and Nirvana will grow up praying to you the way some children pray to the Virgin Mary. Are you a virgin still? You never say.

Yours in remembrance,
Mona

7/5/76

Dear Ellen,

Did you go to the Mall for the fireworks? Did your mother go? I saw part of it on the TV news and the press of people looked overwhelming. Do you remember the year your mother took us and that kid she felt sorry for, Katie somebody, to the fireworks, only we went to the Tidal Basin and sat under the cherry trees? There was a woman nearby whose purse got stolen and a bunch of guys chased the thief and it was all so wholesome that we cheered when he got caught. Then the guys beat him bloody.

Erasmus and I got to see our fireworks from the river. My boss took us in a canoe on the Missouri River. His canoe club does this every year. That's such a funny notion to me, being in a canoe *club*, having an official *club* for canoe-ers. I asked him, Steve, my boss, if they had secret passwords and handshakes, but he just looked at me oddly. He doesn't laugh at what I say because I think he thinks everything I say has significance. He's always telling me how meaningful I am. It's funny to be taken seriously by somebody so square. Steve won't tell me his age but he's got to be old, maybe forty, and he wears his hair in long ringlets over his collar and he has a mustache that droops down the sides of his cheeks. He looks just like some historical relative of his in the Civil War. He showed me the picture and it was uncanny how the two of them could have traded places. He's got a wife who's uninteresting, he says, and three kids, although I can't imagine that because he's so uncool with Erasmus, all *ga-ga* over Erasmus, like he's the kid of the Japanese emperor.

Erasmus is in the terrible twos now. I told Steve that, and he said, Yeah, just wait. Next there's the horrible threes and then the fucked-up fours and on and on. He didn't seem real optimistic about kids. What can you expect about a guy who doesn't take his own boys to the fireworks? All the other women in the canoes were wives, lots older than me, responsible kinds of women who know how to make potato salad and how to defrost freezers. They helped me show Erasmus how to pee over the side of the canoe. The wives were nice to me in a surprised kind way. It was because of Erasmus. They are loyal to any woman with a small child. Erasmus is turning into such an odd little kid. He's glum. He acts like I'm too crazy for the both of us, like I've used up all the craziness he could ever dare be. He eats antibiotics the same as candy because of his ear infections. I've lost count of the nights Erasmus and I've stayed up because of his ears. We listen to AM radio. You know how when it's after midnight you can get faraway stations that buzz and pop. We do ballroom dancing in the kitchen. It's just the two of us. We are constant companions. Sometimes I can half-close my eyes and look at his doughy, pouty little face, and I can see his grown-up face, the bones of it, inside him. Sometimes when he has a tantrum he flails and shrieks, all red and sweaty and dangerous like a demon, and I step back from it and just watch. I stop yelling or whatever brought it on; I just observe, and I see how it's his soul he's struggling with. He's mostly a beast, a wild animal snapping at whatever hurts, but inside he's got this nugget of consciousness being born and it's a lot of what hurts. It's his destiny to be human and he fights because it's painful. My grown-up loneliness and confusion pale next to his struggle. Instead I am knocked over by this fierce, demanding love that shoots out of my gut like a projectile. He is part of my soul as much as he is part of my body. Think of that. A part of my soul broke off and enveloped itself in flesh and is going now independently into the world. I can *see* him, Erasmus, as a man, inside the grimy, weepy little boy. That's why the scandalized wives were nice to me. They know Steve is a creep and that I'm probably a creep for messing around with him. But we mothers have got these little broken-off pieces of soul we're responsible for. We've got that in common and it transcends the other social codes.

Someday I want to go dancing with Erasmus, when he is taller than I am and stronger and more mature. It's easy to see he will grow more mature than I am. Please remind me, Ellen, twenty years from now. You are my memory bank. I forget all these things as soon as the envelope to you is sealed because I trust you completely with my life. You are a better one to hold it than I ever will be.

With fierce, demanding love,
Mona

1/13/83
Dear Ellen,

Merry Christmas! I am instituting a new tradition called the Post-Holiday Greeting. There's a market, I know, among those who do not send cards, who do not participate in the madness and then suffer after it's over. I should have baked turkeys for a shelter and decorated cookies for a children's hospital. I should have gone to a concert of the Messiah and a living nativity at church. I should have gotten my husband something more than drugstore aftershave. I should have wrapped it in gold-foil paper instead of the Sunday funnies. I should have put a wreath on the door. Hell, I should have put a thousand lights and an inflatable Santa on the roof. I should have lived. One more Christmas joins the nostalgic past and I forgot to live it. That's what I think even as OP (Other People's) cards invade my mailbox with images of home fires and fruitcake and cute Christmas mice whose lives are more festive than my own. (I notice your card did *not* invade my mailbox. After all these years, have you given up on me? Or have you, too, resigned from the rush? My Post-Holiday Greeting will suit your new lifestyle.)

I forgive you for not sending me a card. Actually, you probably sent one and it boomeranged. In the two years since I last wrote I moved three times officially (meaning the post office knows) and twice unofficially. I changed my name twice. In '82 I divorced Dave and took back my maiden name. Three months later I married Jesus Bienvenidos, and in a moment of weakness took his name. I love his name. You would like him, but you would not approve of him. He is from Cuba and has three children by an illegal immigrant from El Salvador. He has a band that plays Latin Rockabilly, and he works in the day installing burglar alarms for upwardly-mobile yuppies who can't quite afford their new, overly large houses. If Jesus and I get desperate, we know the alarm systems and floor plans for dozens of easily robbable places.

I'm still in sales. I starved during the recession, but things are hot as a firecracker now. I wholesale a tony brand of organic shampoos to beauty shops. We have hair-care products for all the money in your pocketbook. My own hair is short and red. I mousse it straight up. It makes me look excited.

Are you still living with your mom? I told you two years ago you should go back to grad school. You'd love it. You have the perfect situation for it, no rent, no kids, no career. You'd be happy as a pig in mud, reading wonderful books all day and debating with aged-hippie professors. Actually, you probably have your Ph.D. by now and I've lost track.

My boys are with Dave. I couldn't afford to fight for them, and they're better off with him. They get embarrassed easily, especially Erasmus. He's nine now, and a raving Junior Republican. He called me last week and was talking about trickle-down economics, and I made a crack about voodoo economics. He got all snitty, so I told him his real daddy used to do real voodoo. Well! If the voodoo didn't hit the fan! Dave got on the phone and told me a thing or two not worth repeating. I just don't get this motherhood business. I thought you were supposed to be genuine with kids. I had never in my life thought two seconds about what comes out of my mouth until I got kids. With them I have to write a script before I talk.

Anatole has a birthday tomorrow. He'll be three. He still thinks I'm great. I've got a bunch of gifts for him, but I haven't mailed them. The problem is I shipped the boys their Christmas

stuff only last week, so Dave's still mad at me about that. I got
Anatole lots of picture books because he loves hearing stories.
Kid books are different now. Remember when everyone was
white and Mom wore high heels and an apron? Now Mom lives
with her butch girlfriend and the kids have suntans. That's okay,
but they don't have faces. It bothers me how kid books don't
have faces anymore. I was at the library last week. I missed the
boys so I went to the children's library and sat down and read to
any kid that strayed close to me. Most of them got snatched away
by stranger-phobic parents, but a few stayed. I picked old
chestnuts like *Make Way for Ducklings* and *Yertle the Turtle*. The
kids would bring me their favorites, new books that have been
illustrated by people more successful than I am. They must be,
because they see things more boldly and more beautifully than
I do. None of them see faces. The faces are damp, empty spaces,
sometimes with impressions like one might make in clay, but
without features. I saw the same thing at a new beauty shop I'm
wooing. It's a very hip shop, done in black, white, chrome, and
leather. The head shots they hang on the walls, you know, to
show the hair styles, none of them have any faces. The shampoo
girl goes through the magazines. I saw this one day. The
shampoo girl has a discarded pair of trim scissors and she cuts out
the faces from the fashion magazines.

Now I will mail this and pray that it reaches you. I think of you
often, Ellen, in the way some women carry the daily memory of
a lost love. I tell people I went to high school with Chrissie
Hynde, that I knew her before she changed her name, and we
were best friends. When I say that, I am thinking really of you.
With unrequited love,
Mona

3/25/87
Dear Ellen,
I am grieved to hear the sad news about your mother. I liked

her the best of all the mothers of anyone I have ever known. She was kind and charitable, and she listened to me blather without laughing at me. She made me feel loved when I was at an unlovable age. How you must miss that love. How I have envied you, living for years with her generous love. What will we do now, without her?

I am crying. I did not expect to. She is an anchor in my memory. She has never aged since the summer of 1970 when I ran away from home and hid in your basement for two weeks before your mother discovered me, although years later we found out that she had known all along. I remember how it was the middle of the night when she pretended to find me. Your dad was asleep. She made English Breakfast tea in a pot that looked like a plum, and we played checkers at the kitchen table. The windows were open. The curtains trembled in the summer air. No one used air conditioning back then. She asked me what I was going to do with my life and I told her I was going to fuck it up, and that is exactly what I have done.

With sadness,
Mona

8/3/94
Dear Ellen,
Jesus killed himself. He was forty years old. He took a plane to Florida. He walked out on the Gulf beach at two in the morning and shot himself.

The turtle people found him. They patrol the beaches looking for sea-turtle nests. The turtle people were very kind to me. I had to go identify and claim the body. Anatole went with me. He is fourteen now, and he spends the summers with me. He is a great comfort. He is a loving child, very different from Erasmus, who is at William and Mary.

Anatole and I took a flight into Sarasota. We rented a car and drove to Venice. It is a clean, old-fashioned town on an island.

It is filled with vigorous, suntanned, bicycle-riding old people. The turtle people are old. Their faces are full of smile lines and they walk in a busy, successful way. Even on the beach, they walk that way.

Ruth and Homer took us to the place where Jesus killed himself. It was late, after sunset. All evidence of death had been washed away by the ocean. Ruth is a retired biologist and Homer is a retired CPA. They are part of a group trying to save sea turtles by protecting their eggs.

The mother sea turtle crawls onto the beach where she digs a hole and lays one hundred eggs. She cries salt tears from the effort. When she is done, she can barely drag herself back to the ocean. She never sees the babies. All her tremendous maternal sacrifice goes into egg laying. She lays one hundred eggs to insure that one chosen child makes it to adult turtlehood. Only one. The other eggs are dug up and eaten by raccoons. Or they hatch and are devoured by birds of prey during the turtle race for the ocean. Her one precious offspring survives by chance, by winning the lottery of life.

Ruth and Homer want to change the odds. They put wire cages around the nests to keep out coons and foxes and dogs and humans. When the babies hatch, Ruth and Homer escort them to the ocean. Anatole and I got to chaperon the nestlings at the place where Jesus died. That's why the turtle people found Jesus, because they knew the babies were ready to emerge and they checked the site every night.

"Cubans are romantic people," Homer said. "Is this the beach where his family landed?"

I said I thought all the Cubans went through Miami. Jesus's father came to Florida in '51.

"This place meant something to him," Ruth agreed. "Maybe his family lived here a while. Most of the exiles spent time with menial jobs. Maybe this was where his father did janitor work, or something like that, until he could start his dental practice again."

Jesus and I have lived as such rootless, middle-class exiles, that it startled me to think about his dignified father being a janitor, humiliating himself over trash cans and toilet bowls. Jesus cleaned construction trailers once. He said it didn't matter. But he shot himself. I'm glad his parents are dead. They were Catholics, and suicide is a terrible sin. I wonder if Jesus lied about not caring that he was a janitor. I wonder if he lied about not believing church law. I wonder if he died with the knowledge that he was sending himself to hell because he could not bear joining his family in purgatory or seeing his saintly father already crowned in heaven.

"Jesus was romantic," Homer insisted, as though they were friends who had shared confidences. "He shot himself in the heart. Only romantics do that."

The beach where Jesus died is rocky and heaped with sharp-edged, broken shells. The water is green and warm. It rolls on the shore without breaking into waves. Anatole tried to be sad for my sake, but he loved the water at night. He loved the little turtles. They had hatched and were digging out of the sand nest in a frantic group effort. They fit in your palm, and they look prehistoric—ancient, armored beasts, raw with life, unblinking, cold and wet and hard like little stones. The nestlings surged over the brim of their nursery. They swarmed across the sand in a desperate but impersonal quest for the ocean. We guarded them by the white light of the moon. Artificial lamps confuse them. Ruth and Homer let Anatole redirect the lost souls. Normally people are not allowed to touch them. The turtle people do not want to interfere with the instincts that will guide these creatures back home for their own egg laying. I think Ruth and Homer felt sorry for Anatole. They probably thought he was Jesus's son. Do you know that the first year of life for the sea turtle is a mystery? Once they wash into the Gulf they vanish. Nobody knows where they live, what they eat, how they protect themselves.

I went to the newspaper in Venice. It publishes twice a week. I asked that nothing be printed about Jesus's public suicide. They were agreeable although they already had a small piece typeset. Jesus was a stranger. When I saw the paper, it had on the ninth page a startling, blank, white space, one-and-a-half inches square.

That night on the beach, and two days later on the flight out of Sarasota, I looked westward over the Gulf and tried to see with Jesus's eyes. For all I knew of him and shared with him, I could not imagine what he might have seen. His ashes lie in a box. They are indistinguishable from the wood ash in my cold stove, left over from spring. I have forgotten what day that was, most likely in late April, when Jesus built the last fire of the season. When I looked at the placid Gulf, I could imagine only the tiny bodies of baby turtles swimming to save themselves during the lost year of their youth.

Mona

Kevin Canty

The author with tricycle in Berkeley, California, sometime
in the Eisenhower administration (note nifty shirt).

Kevin Canty's first novel, *Into the Great Wide Open*, was published by Nan A. Talese/Doubleday in August. He is also the author of a collection of stories titled *A Stranger in This World* (Doubleday, 1994; Vintage, 1995). His short fiction has appeared in *Esquire*, *Story*, *New England Review*, and *Missouri Review*. Canty teaches writing at the University of Montana in Missoula, where he lives with his wife, Lucy Capeheart, and their children, Turner and Nora.

KEVIN CANTY
Flipper

$\mathcal{S}$omething's gone wrong with the boy. It's easy to see: his face (once lovely, elfin) is cased in a block of suet now. Wings of fat droop over his belt, shiver when he moves. Eleven years old. Little fireplug, roly-poly, mama's little fatty. When he bends to find his shoes, the rolls of flesh on his stomach meet in dolphin lips.

His mother said it and his sister overheard. Now it's just his name: Flipper.

Summer evenings, freeze-tag, fireflies, War, lemonade and sleep before dark. At bedtime, the name of Flipper is called from child to child, through the alleys (creosote and new wood, the smell of fences, everything new and naked), the woods at the end of the road, all the way to the comics-and-candy store on Hudson Avenue where he is trying to make himself disappear. Baby Huey.

Then they are driving all the way to Pennsylvania: his mother, his father, and Flipper. His sisters have been left behind. No one should be forced to see the camp for fat children, none but the punished. A hundred Flippers! Spare the girls! He sits in the backseat, alone, watching the telephone wires gallop from pole to pole, trying to hypnotize himself. Grim necks of his parents.

Glimmer Train Stories, Issue 22, Spring 1997
©1997 Kevin Canty

This is New Jersey, 1964, the cars of the Kennedy assassination. He doesn't dare speak. Flipper is hungry.

At camp, there is no common misery, but a hundred separate ones, no two alike: Baby Huey, Little Lotta, Porky, Tubby, Flipper. They tip the canoes on impact. They stare at their dismal breakfast bowls: oatmeal, plain. They have swimming practice, like giant cabbages tumbled into the water, their noses fill and bleed with green lake. Harmonicas, campfires. In the absence of their everyday tormentors, they quickly organize themselves into bullies and victims, and fight over smuggled Milk Duds. Two boys are caught "fucking" and sent home. There are bedwetters. Flipper has the top bunk. When the counselor shuts the lights off, the room fills with quiet sobs, they sleep on damp pillows. Once in a while, the telltale rustle of wax paper. All ears alert.

One day Flipper goes for a walk in the forest. The counselors call it "hiking." Alone: the fat campers are solitary, each encased in each. Ridiculous in shorts, and knowing it—his legs are pink as pigskin despite weeks of sun—he clambers over logs, hops from rock to rock to cross the creek. He dreams that this path will lead him to a Rexall store, a place of comic books and candy, an hour of comfort. His soft and secret heart. Lies on the bank of the creek in the morning sun and feels the warm grass springing upright again, tickling his neck. Almost time to go back. He pictures his lunch: an orange dome of canned cling peach on top of white cottage cheese, like a mockery of a fried egg. Fried eggs! And dry toast, when all he dreams of is butter, butter and Heath bars and marshmallow Easter chicks. Bitter and small and hard. The idea takes shape in his brain then, a wisp of smoke and then the hazy outline, and then the idea: He is not going back.

Dead by the road. Anywhere. You'll be sorry.

He doesn't run, he *couldn't* run. The stumps and switchy branches reach to trip him, the smell of skunk cabbage fills the marshy bottoms like a gigantic fart racing after him. Poor Flipper! They will picture this escape when he's dead. They will see they were wrong. The emptiness inside him, the place where lunch ought to be, and snacks, and the love of his mother, and softness, and sleeping—this empty place contracts and loosens around a burning core. Damaged organ. Unlovely wobbling. After half an hour he heaves himself over the last fence of the camp and into the forbidden world.

His skin is covered with a fine, damp sheen of sweat and his thighs are starting to chafe a little. Dying will be even worse. He fights back tears, girl-tears. The lumps of flesh on his chest, his father called them man-tits. A girl, an ugly girl, a fat girl. Flipper does not need a tormentor. He does not need help.

In an opening in the forest, not far from the lake, he comes across a girl who is also weeping. The terror of being looked at stops his own tears, the distant, longed-for call to heroism.

Are you lost? he asks, stepping out of the trees.

She shakes her head, still nestled in her arms and her knees, won't give him anything. Her voice comes muffled through her dress: Go away!

I don't know where I am, he says.

Well, go away anyway!

He stands rooted in the meadow. She weeps again, head shaking, burrowing into her dress. It's checkered red-and-white, like a tablecloth. Screaming, splashing from the lake, the other children having fun, the ones from the Baptist camp, the Boy Scout camp, the rich camp. Her hair is blond and cut abruptly at the neck, and on her neck are two small red spots, remains of pimples, so she's older. Is something wrong? he asks her.

This time she looks up, and her face is swollen and round and covered with pimples new and old, and she is enormously pregnant. How could she draw her knees up around that belly? The dress concealed her. Two years older than Flipper, maybe thirteen. Her belly rests between her legs like an enormous stone she has swallowed. I hurt my baby! she wails. I didn't mean to!

What?

Can't answer; not now. Buries her face in her dress again and weeps, head shaking, clasping her hands so tight that her fingernails make white moons in her palms. Can you do that? Flipper wonders. Can you make yourself bleed? Thirteen and pregnant. He's never thought about that. Opens her face to him again and says, You won't tell anyone?

No.

Opens her dress and a lapful of candy spills out, all chocolate, little Halloween bars of everything: Hershey's, Nestle's, Peter Paul Mounds. He can't stop staring, though her lap is nothing he should be seeing, the primitive bulge under the silvery brown candy. She says, They told me not to but I couldn't help it. I'm so bad. They told me not to for my baby!

The silence, wind in the trees and the splashing, screaming, happy children, voices torn into the wind like scattered paper. You're all right, he says. You didn't do anything bad.

Miranda!

The voice comes distantly through the forest, then closer, the adult voice, counselors, footprints breaking on the brittle leaves. Take these! she says, all frightened, pushing the candy into his hands, scooping the little silvery bits into his greedy hands. Flipper is rich! Ten or twenty little candies, they overstuff his pockets, he looks down and sees the tops of her breasts through the loose top of her dress, blue veined and milky white. Now go! she says, and Flipper goes.

Watches from the edge of the little clearing. A nun and then another nun come out, say something he can't hear. The full dress-model nun, with the hats and so on. Flipper squats, terrorized, Jesus will point him out, radio under the starched headdress, radar, they know, they have to know. Still he can't help following when they leave with her. A nun, the pregnant

girl, another
nun, like pris-
oners in a war
movie. Pockets
crammed with
candy, he steals
through the

woods, following the white flash of the nuns and the red of her
dress, a safe distance behind. Looking for what? He won't tell
himself. Pizza face, preggy, the bulgy, blue-veined skin. Not far
from disgust, not far from himself. Pasty-white, fatty, Baby
Huey. White-frame houses through the trees, he thrashes closer,
breaking twigs. Nobody notices him.

Through the scrap and scrub at the edge of the forest he
sees green lawns, green shutters, porches, a swimming pool.
Chaise lounges on the lawn, a pregnant girl in a swimming suit
in each, six or eight, but he's not counting. Some kind of
treatment? They aren't happy, they aren't talking. These are
the two-piece kind of bathing suits, so their bellies shine like
moons in the light. Flipper wants to cry. On the porches, on the
lawns, are pregnant girls, in bathing suits or tent-dresses, one
modeled after a sailor's suit, navy blue with white piping ... and
the nuns, like moving telephone booths, walking on invisible
legs, keeping track. Guarding against pleasure or happiness.
They lead Miranda into one of the buildings and then, a few
minutes later, lead her out again, this time wearing a bathing suit
herself. They lead her to a lounge and she lies on her back, with
her eyes closed but not sleeping. Not wanting to see. The blue
veins stand out clearly on her breasts, the part he can see, and on
her thighs. Humiliation. He watches from the edge of the forest
until he gets a feeling: she knows he is there, knows he is
watching. Then turns, and starts back for the fat camp.

What kind of boy is Flipper? He hides his treasure in a hollow tree, a hundred yards from camp, though squirrels might find it. The little bars are soft from carrying them in the pocket of his shorts, almost melted from the damp heat of Flipper. He allows himself one, a Hershey's, soft as velvet on his tongue. Leaves the lump of chocolate in his mouth, lets it melt to nothing. Bliss. He closes his eyes, feels the sunlight on his skin. A face in the darkness. Hair as soft and blond as a baby's, No More Tears. She was fucking, really fucking, there is no other explanation; the thought makes him tremble. She had outgrown the small sins of children. Someday soon, he thinks. No More Tears. Holding the chocolate in his mouth, not swallowing until the last taste melts away, eyes closed, concentrating. Then licks the wrapper clean.

Tells the counselors that he fell asleep in the woods. Either they believe him or they don't care.

The counselors were never fat. The counselors have beautiful, tanned bodies, they watch each other, the children disappear. Lesser species. Burning ants with a magnifying glass.

Canned cling-peach halves for dessert, cold from the refrigerator, they taste like refrigerator.

I'm not supposed to, Miranda says. They say it makes my baby excited.

It can't hurt anything, Flipper says. It's just a little bit.

I don't want to do anything to hurt my baby.

You don't have to, Flipper says, if you don't want to.

This time it's Special Dark. Slowly he unwraps the paper, then the foil, and slips the little sharp-edged square into his mouth, still cool and hard from a night in the forest. This time he carried it in a bag so it wouldn't melt. Ten thirty in the morning, hazy blue sky, the sun warming toward the dust and emptiness of the afternoon. He closes his eyes but she doesn't go away, and in a minute he hears the rustle of the bag, the snap of a paper wrapper opening. He brought three for himself and three for her. No hurry. They have all morning. The edges soften, bittersweet.

There! she says. You can feel him, there! She guides his hand to the lower curve of her belly, presses her own hand over his. Through the soft cotton of her dress, he can feel her taut skin, bulging, ready to burst. She smells of soap and milk and medicine. Suddenly he feels it, the soft bone turning deep inside her, the baby. Instinct tries to pull his hand away, but she presses down, holds it close, and this time he feels a stronger shove, an elbow or a knee, something alive in there! A person inside you, Flipper thinks. A person inside me. His hand on her belly, inches away from her breasts, inches away from where she pees from, where the baby will come spilling out not long from now. Disgust and fascination mixed. The sweets well up inside him, and still he can't take his hand away. She won't let him, anyway.

He doesn't like it when I eat chocolate, Miranda says.

She's there again the next day, and the next.

At weigh-in Sunday morning, it turns out Flipper's lost three pounds, champion of the week. His cabin gets pizza that night. He dares to dream about her. Special Dark, he's been saving them: three for her and three for him. Flipper will lie next to her in the grass, eyes closed, both of them. Lying alone on his hard little bunk, he can feel the morning sunlight on his skin, tickle of damp grass. With his eyes closed, Flipper sees the milk white and porcelain blue of her breasts, she's careless with them. Once he saw her right down to the nipple. Two bunks away, a boy is sobbing in the darkness. The wind is churning the leaves of the trees outside, a sound like rain. Right down to the nipple. He opens his eyes to the darkness of the cabin, and imagines that she meant for him to see her.

In the morning it is raining. Two days until it will end. He stays away from the tree, to save the last of the Special Dark. When the third day comes up sunny, he barely finishes his breakfast. Miranda has been with him each night, growing inside him. He has dared to dream about her.

At the tree he finds a litter of foil and wrappers on the ground, nothing in the hollow. Another camper has been here.

Flipper shrinks again, pathetic. A cheap sound like a crying baby doll bubbles out of his thick, stupid body, and scalding tears. Flipper is the fattest and the stupidest. Miranda has big zits all over her face. He can't go see her empty-handed, but the camp store sells only wholesome snacks, nothing she would love, nothing for them to share. The nearest real chocolate is in the country store, three or four miles away, the rumor says. It might as well be Mercury. He can feel her in the sunlight, how she would turn her face toward the sun, eyes closed, like some vine twisting toward the light. Gone and gone. Flipper is discarded, weeping trash bag.

Now Flipper is hurrying down the shoulder of the road. Now Flipper is running. Big trucks are driving by, inches from his feet. It doesn't matter what happens to him.

For love, he thinks, oh, love. The word comes into his mind at an angle, like another language, because it's the wrong word. What he really wants is this: he wants her to look up at him when he comes into the clearing, he wants her to see the big bar of chocolate in his hands, wants her to know that he had gone especially for her, all the way to the country store, way out in the forbidden world, the dangerous world, and brought this back for her. He wants to see her eat as much as she wants. He wants the smear of melted chocolate on her lips.

Hero.

Now Flipper is trying not to cry again. The counselors caught up to him while he was in the country store, or maybe the bitch behind the counter called the camp on him. She has a hatchet face: bitch. They joke back and forth. This isn't the first time. While she's laughing, Flipper backs up to the candy counter, slips a book-size slab of Special Dark into his underwear. No one will notice. His shorts are enormous. He can feel the waxy wrapper, cool against the skin of his ass, and then it melts and shapes itself to him.

Kid Galahad, the counselor says, driving back. She sees the crafty look in his pig eyes.

He's grounded for a week, confined to cabin. His parents are written. He carefully straightens the bar of Special Dark back into a rectangle during the hot afternoons alone, in the sunlight next to his cot. He can feel her in the sunlight. He can feel her inside him. He practices in whispers, moving his lips, I brought this for you. I got this at the country store.

Now Flipper is standing alone in the little clearing. The sound of an outboard motor rings up from the lake, splashing, swimming, aluminum canoes. She isn't there.

He'll come again tomorrow, and the day after. He will come every week for the rest of the summer but she will not be there. Miranda's gone to have her baby.

Flipper knows this right away. The clearing is empty. Flipper is a big stupid baby.

He lies on his side in the grass. He sees himself from above, like he was already dead. Trash bag. He puts his hand on the bare skin of his own soft stomach, remembering the tight-stretched skin under the thin cloth. He touches his tiny dick. He saw her once, right down to the nipple. He takes the chocolate bar out of the bag, unwraps the waxy paper and the foil, breaks off a little jagged triangle and slips it in his mouth, no hurry, he's got all afternoon, he's got the whole thing to himself. But the taste is wrong, or the feel of it in his mouth, maybe from the melting and unmelting, but it tastes like breakfast food, or sawdust. She isn't coming. He eats the whole bar anyway, slowly, like it was his duty. Dust, sunlight, aluminum canoes, the grass against his neck. He finishes the chocolate and wads the wrapper up into a ball and stands up, a little dizzy from the sugar, but the empty place inside him is still empty. He wants, he wants, he wants, an open mouth and nothing more. Flipper is still hungry.

Alice Mattison

*The dog was named Skippy. I'm holding him. My sister Emily,
now called Savita, is looking at the camera—and at my mother
behind it. Usually my father photographed us, but he's in this one.*

"Sebastian Squirrel" is from a collection of intersecting stories, *Men Giving Money, Women Yelling*, which will be published by William Morrow in July. Alice Mattison is also the author of the novel *Hilda and Pearl*, three previous books of fiction, and a collection of poems. Her stories have appeared in *The New Yorker*, *Boulevard*, *The North American Review*, *The New England Review*, and elsewhere.

ALICE MATTISON
Sebastian Squirrel

*W*hen Ida and I decided to get married we didn't know how to go about it, but my boss, John Corey, said, "The lawyer with the downstairs toilet is a judge now. Judges marry people." At first I didn't understand, because I didn't call her The Lawyer With the Downstairs Toilet, even though John and I had built her a half-bath next to her kitchen. I called her the First Breast-Feeding Lady. When John, who is my sister Barbara's husband, hired me to help in his business—carpentry and renovations— the judge's was the first house we worked on together. She had a new baby then, and she breast-fed him all day long. I loved it. This is not just Lustful Tom sneaking looks at a breast. I had reverence for those breasts: reverence as a sexual man, yes, but also as a new adult, a new member of what I considered a club whose members were all the grown-ups, and whose task was to see to all of the children. I couldn't get over it that women made milk and babies sucked it out.

Ida thought it was a fine idea to be married by "one of Tom's beautifully installed toilets," as she put it. I felt shy, because the Breast-Feeding Lady had been so important in my imagination that it was hard to think of her as a particular person with her blouse buttoned. By this time, though, the baby would be a little kid and the lady would be like anybody, except that she was a judge, a completely different sort of particular person. So I called her. Ida and I had decided to be married at our favorite spot in Edgerton Park, not far from where we live: a flat, grassy place near a stone fountain at the top of a hill. "Even if it rains," Ida insisted.

The judge remembered me. She said she'd be happy to marry us. "But when?" she said. "I'm having a baby."

"You already had one," I said.

"Oh, I want a pair."

The wedding was two months off, in the summer, and she said that would be fine. The baby would be a few weeks old by that time. "I know it's a girl," she said. "All right if I bring her? I nurse my babies often."

"Sure," I said. "But it could rain."

"Babies like rain."

Ida was delighted about the baby. She felt strongly that our wedding should be just one of the things we did the day we got married, and she wanted everything about it to be as ordinary as possible.

"So do I go to work and get married on my lunch hour?" I said.

"No, you can take the day off," she said. "And of course my mother and Aunt Freddie will come from Rochester, and your family will be there, and so forth. We'll go out to lunch after the ceremony. But in the morning, let's buy groceries or work in the garden." We had just moved in together, in an apartment on Orange Street, and the landlord said we could plant things.

"Once I was a bridesmaid," Ida said. "I hated it. It took three days for that woman to get married, and none of us did anything *but* get her married. The dinner the night before. The brunch the day after. I had to wear an itchy, light green, dopey dress made for skinny people." Ida is magnificently fat.

I wondered how Sally, Ida's mother, would feel about going to the supermarket with us the morning of our wedding, and sure enough, she and Ida had discussions on the phone.

"Rehearsal dinner?" I heard Ida say once, with a hoot. "*Rehearsal?* Oh, give me a break." Then, "Oh, I suppose Kitty can stand up with me." Kitty was Ida's roommate before we lived together.

"My mother is so timid," Ida said when she hung up. "She lets me be rotten to her."

"That doesn't mean you have to be!" I said. Ida had told her mother she wasn't wearing any goddamn bridal gown.

"She wanted to talk about whether 'white is appropriate,'" said Ida, her voice getting whispery as she quoted her mother. "She wanted to talk about 'ecru.'"

My mother had asked me whether I was going to rent a tux. "What *are* we going to wear?" I said to Ida.

She shrugged. In the end she bought a dark pink skirt, very long and wide and terrific, and a funky white shirt with tucks and loose sleeves. Then I got interested and found a comparable white shirt, also with tucks. We'd look fine, we just wouldn't look like a wedding. We'd walk hand in hand to the park in our tucked shirts.

The morning of our wedding, I woke up in my old bed at my parents' house, much too early. It wasn't quite an ordinary day after all: we'd lent our bed to Sally and Aunt Freddie. But waking up at my parents' place felt right, like stepping backwards before jumping forward. Birds I never knew about sang for hours in the dark and then in the funny light. When it was late enough to call Ida I did. She'd been up too, on the sofa. We had the kind of good talk we had on the phone before we lived together. We discussed all the habitual breakfasts of our lives, and the things we never ate for breakfast. Whenever we talked like this, first we'd discuss our childhoods in detail, and I loved that. But Ida is six years older than I am; we first knew each other when she was my teacher in high school, so my teenage years are embarrassing to talk about. Worse are the years before we found each other again—the people we were with by mistake, like wrong numbers on the phone. Once Ida had an affair with a man who ate soup for breakfast.

Finally we decided that I'd come over right away and stop for bagels, though the night before, Sally had said, "It's bad luck for the groom to see the bride on the day of the wedding."

I didn't like the word "groom."

Ida said, "Oh, Jews don't think like that," and Sally said, "But you're being married by a judge."

Later I saw Sally standing by herself near the window. She was saying in a low voice, "Of *course* Jewish people think like that!" I knew she didn't want me around in the morning because she wanted her daughter to herself one last time, even though Ida hadn't lived with her for years. I couldn't stay away, but I felt bad about it. We love the ones we love and I don't know why it has to be a matter of discussion. I don't know why I had to wait to grow up to get Ida. I don't know why everyone can't have whomever they love. Oh, I guess I do know.

At our apartment that morning, baskets of laundry were in the living room and the book Ida was reading was open on the arm of a chair, hanging down to keep her place. Tapes waited

J. LEON 96

36

near the stereo to be put back into their cases. I was surprised for a second that we hadn't done anything about all this. It seemed that the day before you get married you ought to clean your house, put the tapes away, and finish the book you were reading. But no, it was an ordinary day, just as we'd said, and on second thought I liked that better.

When I came in with the bagels I heard voices in the kitchen. "Turbulence!" Aunt Freddie was saying. She wore a red bathrobe. She was drinking coffee and stabbing the table with her finger. She is not Ida's mother's sister, but her father's sister—he died years ago—and she's big like Ida, but with white hair. Sally is little and keeps her hands close to her body.

Ida was drinking coffee too. "Aunt Freddie says we need wildness in our lives," she said. "Maybe getting married is too easy."

"I don't care," I said.

"When I was thirty," said Aunt Freddie, "I thought I might marry a man in my office."

"I never knew that!" said Ida. "I never knew you even considered getting married."

"Oh, yes," said Aunt Freddie. "I picked him out, and I waited for him to think of marrying me. He worked down the hall. One morning I decided I ought to check several times a day with the receptionist, to see if I had messages. I'd have had to walk past him each time. Then I saw what I was up to. The messages could wait! I asked to work on a different floor, and I got fat on purpose. From then on I spent every vacation in the kind of foreign country you can't go to without awful shots. In between I thought about my next vacation." She reached into the bag for a bagel.

"But why?" I said. I liked the thought of a woman walking past a man, hoping. I didn't think anyone had ever walked past me that way.

Aunt Freddie stood, as if an answer should be made from a

standing position, or maybe she just wanted to cut the bagel standing up. "I am a lover of time and chance," she said.

"Time?" I said.

"Time will talk to you," she said, "but not if everything has already been decided."

"What does time say?" said Ida, like a little girl at story hour.

"It says, 'Now.'" Freddie whispered the last word. She raised a finger, urging us to listen, and I thought maybe time had just spoken, but it was the sound of the shower. "Sally's up," she said.

"I wish I'd thought all this through sooner," said Ida.

"But we love each other," I said.

"Of course there's that too," said Aunt Freddie. "Where are the rings?"

"Don't you want a bagel, Tom?" Ida said just then, and Aunt Freddie found that extremely funny, as if we were going to use bagels for rings, so Ida put a bagel on her finger and marched up and down the kitchen, singing, "Here comes the bride, All dressed in white, Here comes the fella, All dressed in yella …" Ida was wearing a long white T-shirt she liked to sleep in—she really *was* dressed in white—and she looked great. Her hair is thick and blond and hangs over her back and shoulders. But then she stopped and said, "But where *are* the rings?"

"Didn't you put them in your bag?" I said.

"I took them out," said Ida. "Weren't they here on the counter?"

Sometimes when things were put onto the counter, they'd fall into a drawer just below it, and Ida and I started removing wooden spoons, spatulas, and the egg beater from that drawer. When Sally came in, we hadn't found the rings, but we had stopped to eat bagels. Sally said, "I hope you don't mind that I took a shower." She was wearing a fuzzy pink robe and a towel around her head.

"Mother," said Ida, "you know that's the kind of remark I don't like."

"I don't see why," said Sally. "For all I know, you don't have much hot water and you were planning to take a shower yourself."

"I'm not *planning* a shower."

"You're going to get married all sweaty?"

"I didn't say that," said Ida. "But I don't sit down and make plans. I'll take a shower when I feel like it."

Sally looked as if she were trying to figure out how never to make Ida mad again as long as she lived. She didn't eat anything until Ida poured orange juice and coffee for her and cut a bagel in half.

"I can't think where else to look," Ida said, eating the last of her own bagel and standing up.

"You still can't find them?" said Aunt Freddie.

"Find what?" said Sally.

"Oh, the rings," Ida said. "I've lost the rings, but it's just as well. I don't think I want to get married. Getting married is *nothing* but making plans. Planning to sleep with the same guy all your life, planning to live where he lives ..."

"We do love each other," I said. I didn't think maybe we weren't getting married. I wanted to get married, I'd wanted it all along, and I figured it would happen.

"See," said Ida. "I've lost the rings. Unconsciously, I don't want to get married."

"You don't want to get married?" Sally said now.

"She doesn't mean it," I said.

"Of course I mean it!" said Ida.

Now Sally pushed her chair back and stopped eating. "Do you want me to call people and tell them not to come?" she asked. We'd invited about twenty people to the ceremony in the park.

"What people?" said Ida, who was emptying all the drawers, even though things accidentally fell into only one.

"The guests. Don't you and Tom want to be alone so you can discuss this? Shouldn't Freddie and I go to a motel?"

"Oh, Sally. They're getting married!" Freddie said.

Ida swept dish towels and pot holders back into drawers. "I can't think!" she said.

I put my hand on Sally's hand. "Don't worry," I said. "We're getting married." We finally found the rings in Ida's big floppy turquoise bag, where things often disappeared for long periods. She had never taken them out, and had carried them everywhere for a week, which proved she wanted to marry me.

Ida and I had planned to walk to the park—we did plan that much—but Sally and Aunt Freddie decided to drive, because Sally was wearing tricky shoes. "It looks like rain," she said. "And, Ida, are you sure it's legal to have weddings in the park?"

Ida interrupted herself while giving directions to Aunt Freddie, who was going to drive my car. "I reserved the spot," she said to her mother.

"How do you reserve a spot in a park?"

"I called the city," Ida said. "They said sure, go ahead, they love weddings. I suppose they were just relieved it wasn't a mugging we wanted to hold in the park."

"I guess that's so," said Sally.

All of a sudden I couldn't help mussing my small, future mother-in-law's hair. "Why did you do that, Tom?" she said, stepping back and looking up at me. She was wearing a blue dress that looked big on her. She has short gray hair that hangs down on either side of her face. She looked even smaller than usual.

"I like you," I said, and she stared at me, and blushed, but then she looked happy.

When Ida and I—both in our splendid shirts, Ida in her dark pink skirt—reached the pretty place at the top of the hill in the park, holding hands, a fine rain was in the air; Sally was standing in the grass in her high heels with one hand on Freddie's arm, looking frightened; the judge was coming over the hill from the opposite direction in a gray suit, a baby strapped to her chest and accompanied by a man pushing a stroller with a little boy in it, while several teenage kids wearing face paint and furry tails and leotards danced and stopped, danced and stopped on the green sloping lawn. For a second I thought they were a kind of wedding present, like people in gorilla suits who bring balloons.

"We're not quite ready," said a wild-haired woman I didn't know, coming toward us. Then she said, "We figured on kids. Do you mind sitting on the grass?"

The judge's little boy climbed out of his stroller. "How come you have a tail?" he asked one of the passing teenagers.

"I'm a raccoon," she said. "Did you come to see the play?"

"I came to get married," said the little boy.

The wild-haired woman said, "We can't start for about half an hour."

Then Ida said, "We're not here to see a play. We're having a wedding."

"Is that part of the festival?" said the woman. "Wasn't there a play in New York that was somebody's wedding?"

"No," said Ida. "I'm getting married. This is my husband."

I didn't like "groom," but I loved "husband." I stepped forward and introduced myself to the woman, whose name was Marta Lowenstein. Eventually it became clear that the friendly office at the city that said we could get married on top of this hill had also arranged for Marta to put on a play there—same time, same place—with dancing and singing and a sign language interpreter.

"The characters are animals actually found in New Haven's parks," Marta Lowenstein said. "We've been touring the parks all summer." Ida looked interested and Marta kept talking. "But I saw precisely *one* poster. I should have done the publicity myself." She was disappointed that we weren't audience. For a while she thought that the judge and her family, at least, were audience, but we had to tell her that they too were present for our sakes.

The rain stopped. Members of the cast kept arriving. Some of them knew Ida from school. When they found out why we were there, they said they wanted to attend Ms. Feldman's wedding. Ida grinned and hugged them.

"We definitely had this place reserved," Sally said.

"What difference does it make?" Ida said. "Maybe the play is good." Musicians arrived and began practicing—three teenagers with flute, violin, and drum. "This is wonderful!" Ida said to Marta.

"I'm glad somebody appreciates it," said Marta. "I've worked my tail off, and at the last park only three people showed up."

"Oh, did you have a tail too?" I said, but nobody noticed except Aunt Freddie, who laughed her deep laugh at me.

The judge seemed to think it was her responsibility to sort everything out. She stepped forward, the baby's little legs and feet dangling from the blue cloth carrier on her chest. The baby's head came just to the top of it. Now she was making little occasional peeps, and when she peeped, the judge danced back and forth to get her back to sleep. "This is complicated," she explained to Ida and Marta and me. "If I nurse Jane now, she'll cry afterwards, but if I get her to sleep a little longer, she won't. I don't know why, but it always happens." While the judge danced, she and Marta decided that they'd hold the play first and then the wedding.

"But do we have time for all this?" said the judge's husband.

"Sure," said the judge. "It's nice for Harry." Harry was the little boy.

By now our guests were arriving. Ida explained to each of them what was going on. My boss, John, arrived with my sister and *their* baby, Carolee, who looked big compared to Jane, the judge's baby. They came up the hill looking happy, with my parents behind them. John clapped me hard on the back and gave me an envelope, which I put into my pocket. His brothers arrived—one of them is gay and his boyfriend came, too—and I received more envelopes. John was my best man and I gave him the rings to hold. Marta Lowenstein greeted one of John's brothers, whom she knew from someplace.

Now Kitty, Ida's maid of honor, came along with her boyfriend. She thought what was happening was terribly funny. She tried to cheer up Sally.

The flutist shyly came up to me and Ida, and offered to play at our wedding, and when we accepted, the musicians went off to practice "Here Comes the Bride." And at last an audience for the play—intending to see the play—showed up: a woman with two little kids. They were speaking a foreign language, maybe Korean. By now some of the raccoons and so forth were giving out programs, and everybody sat down on the part of the hill that felt like the audience. Ida and I held hands. The actors withdrew.

"I keep worrying about that baby," said Sally, who was sitting next to us. The judge's baby had gone back to sleep, still tied to her mother's chest. The judge and her family were just behind us.

"What's wrong with the baby?" said Ida.

"I'm sure that baby is going to suffocate," Sally said. "It's not safe for them to hang off their mothers like that."

The judge's husband was standing closer to Sally than she must have realized, looking for the best spot for his little boy, and I saw him get upset. He was tall, and he kept looking around, in eyeglasses that seemed to glint more than other people's glasses, as if the light were different up where he was. Now he turned to us. "Look, I'm not some sort of idiot!" he said.

Sally turned around. "Well, you don't *look* like an idiot," she said.

"Well, good," he said sarcastically. "Because I'm not. That baby is not suffocating, because I'm her father!"

"Oh, good," said Sally, but the judge's husband, enraged, put his hands on her shoulders and actually shook her.

"I'm making a point!" he said.

"Yes?" said Sally, looking up at him. With her short straight gray hair she looked like an elderly child being shaken by this big man. We were all so surprised that nobody did anything.

Then he stopped and took his hands off Sally and backed away. "Sorry," he said. "Sorry! Tired of old ladies telling me ..."

"Ida!" said Sally. "He assaulted me!"

"Did you assault this woman?" said the judge, who'd been fussing with Harry.

But the play was starting. Pretty young women in tails were running toward us from a grove a short distance away, and the flute and violin and drum were playing. The sign language interpreter stood by herself on the other side of the stage area, looking expectant. As the first song was beginning, I heard sounds and turned around, and the judge's husband, sitting right behind Sally, was trying to give her some money. Maybe he was afraid she'd sue him. "No, really, I owe you something," he said. "I shouldn't have—"

"Shhh!" Ida said.

"Take your daughter to lunch on me. Take her out for a drink," he whispered loudly. He persisted until he'd stuffed a bill into the pocket of Sally's dress. She kept moving away from him as if he were one of those dogs who thinks he's going to bite you and suddenly decides he'd rather lick you all over.

The play was called *Sebastian Squirrel*, and it was about a crafty, wicked, alluring squirrel, played by a talented actor, a black girl with something sad about her. She had a clear, unsettling voice, and she sang a strange song over and over while the flute played in the background—something like, "Who I am, where I'm from ... if only you knew ... if only you knew ..."

The play began with two chipmunks on their way to do their laundry. They were funny, dragging an enormous bag of laundry, arguing and clowning around. Along came the squirrel, and he lured one of the chipmunks away from the other. He had a doll that he'd stolen, and he danced with the doll while the lost, frightened, boy chipmunk danced behind him, imitating just what he did. Then Sebastian Squirrel sang about money, and how much he wanted the chipmunk's money. The audience was supposed to shout and warn the chipmunk, while the chipmunk kept misunderstanding what was being said, turning around and looking for the squirrel in the wrong place. We were a fine audience, and we shouted and shouted—in vain, of course. Finally the chipmunk leaned over, looking for the squirrel near the ground, and the squirrel sneaked up behind him and snatched an enormous ten dollar bill from his picket.

It was a nice play, and nobody was impatient for it to end. The squirrel led the lost chipmunk back and forth, while the chipmunk sang about his girlfriend, who was off to the side pretending to wash clothes on a rock all this time. In the end, a chorus of animals plotted revenge on the squirrel, and even caught him, but when they tried to inject him with a huge make-believe needle and put him to sleep, he ran away, singing that same strange song, "If only you knew, if only you knew ..." It was the kind of song that made you think you'd heard it before but had forgotten, although of course you hadn't.

When it was over we clapped hard. We claimed that the girl who played the squirrel would be famous, and we said we'd remember her name. Then the audience wandered around as if it were intermission, including the woman with the two little kids speaking Korean, and the sign-language interpreter, who had gestured away throughout the performance.

We couldn't have our wedding for a while because Jane was now awake, and the judge was breast-feeding her. She sat contentedly under a tree nursing her daughter, her suit jacket tossed over the baby, while I watched out of the corner of my eye. I could hear Jane making squeaky noises as she sucked. When she was done with one breast, the judge rearranged the jacket and nursed her on the other side, and then she buttoned herself back up, handed the baby to her husband, and put on her jacket. He tied the sling, with the baby in it, to his own chest, but the baby cried.

It had started to rain again, just a light mist. At last the judge took Jane and held her against her shoulder with one hand—she was that tiny—while she carried a book in the other hand, and she walked to what had just been the center of the stage. The audience settled down again, the sign-language interpreter got ready—without even asking us—and the three musicians began to play "Here Comes the Bride." John came to stand with me, biting his lips and smiling. Kitty walked toward us from the grove, carrying flowers, grinning in all directions, and then came Ida and her mother, who was giving her away. Sally was walking briskly despite her high heels, and she and Ida were clutching each other's hands. Everybody glistened from the rain. And then we promised to love each other all our lives, and we put on the rings and kissed and it stopped raining. Everybody talked and hugged, and after a while we all separated and went where we were supposed to go. Ida and Marta ran back to exchange phone numbers. They liked each other. Then we went to a restaurant with our guests. As we drove away in my car, with Sally and Aunt Freddie in the backseat, we passed the judge and her husband walking home. He was wearing the baby and she was pushing the stroller. Everybody waved. That reminded Sally of the money he'd stuck into her pocket. He'd given her a twenty. "He said I should buy you lunch, Ida, but we're having lunch with all those people," she said.

"Oh, we'll find something good to do with it."

We had lunch and dancing and a good time all afternoon. I kept fiddling with my ring. In the evening Ida and I left on our honeymoon. We were driving to a bed and breakfast in Massachusetts that night, and traveling north the next day, while Sally and Aunt Freddie were going to spend one more night in our house and fly back to Rochester in the morning. It was cool and I changed out of my wedding shirt and into my regular shirt and my denim jacket. Just before we left, Sally pulled me over and said, "I feel bad about the money that man gave me, Tom. I guess I shouldn't have said the baby was suffocating."

"But what if she *were* suffocating?" I said. "He had no right—"

"She wasn't suffocating," she said. "I think I'd like to donate the money to charity. Do you and Ida have a favorite charity you'd like to give it to?"

"Sure," I said and stuffed the twenty-dollar bill into the pocket of my denim jacket.

Ida and I took our suitcases and hugged Sally and Aunt Freddie and we got into the car. John's brother Eugene and his boyfriend, Albert, had sneaked out of our lunch and written "Just Married" on my car, and Ida loved that. We drove off while Sally and Aunt Freddie stood in the doorway waving, but as soon as we drove around the corner, Ida said, "I forgot the snack."

"What snack?"

"Milk and cookies," said Ida. "I was too excited to eat all day. I'm going to need milk and cookies before we go to sleep. I got a quart of milk and a package of cookies all ready."

"Do you want to go back?" I said.

"No, we'd just have to have more ceremonies of leave-taking and enthusiasm," said Ida.

So we stopped at the Store 24 downtown, just in case there wasn't going to be any milk between us and the bed and breakfast in Massachusetts. Ida sat in the car, and I got out to buy a quart of milk and a package of chocolate-chunk cookies. Outside the store was a thin old man with a cane, begging for money. One lens of his glasses was covered with Scotch tape. He held out his paper coffee cup and I said, "In a minute," because I had to think. In the store I found milk and cookies, and I waited on line while other people paid. Then I paid and went out and I gave the old man the judge's husband's twenty-dollar bill and got back in the car to be married to my good wife Ida.

Lex Williford

This is a "before" picture, Easter, 1963, five kids already practiced at their fake smiles: me, top left, with obligatory butch haircut; my sister Lisa, top right, with auburn bangs; my brother John, bottom right, with carrot-top crew cut; and my redheaded sister Lou, bottom left, as always holding our brother Carl, beautiful blond child, just months before he got sick.

Lex Williford, a Texas native, holds an MFA from the University of Arkansas. The 1994 Shane Stevens Fellow in Fiction at Bread Loaf Writers' Conference and a recipient of a 1993 National Endowment of the Arts fellowship, he was also co-winner of the 1993 Iowa School of Letters Award for Short Fiction for his book, *Macauley's Thumb*. Two stories from that collection, "Macauley's Thumb" and "Hoot's Last Bubble Bath," appeared in *Glimmer Train Stories*. Williford teaches in the MFA program at the University of Alabama.

LEX WILLIFORD
Jesse

In memory of Carl Alan Williford
July 15, 1962 – November 5, 1965

*T*he year my brother Jesse got sick, what we always feared the most were the nosebleeds. Once they got started, my mother could almost never make them stop, holding an old towel or Jesse's blood-soaked pajama tops under his nose for hours sometimes, squeezing his nostrils shut between her forefinger and thumb, praying that she and my father wouldn't have to take him back again to Baylor Hospital. And what we all feared most I also secretly wanted the most, sometimes even prayed for. Almost every night at the beginning, when Jesse was still strong and angry and mean, as I lay in a room all to myself in the house my father designed, built, and would soon lose because of him, I stared up at my plastic models, the few that had survived him, dangling from my mother's white sewing thread, high up, out of Jesse's reach, and sometimes I imagined being able to hit him as hard as I could, in the stomach, in the nose, till he bled.

"Pray for him," Sister Mary Ruth told us kids at Mass every weekday morning before classes at St. Patrick's School. "Pray for *yourselves*," my mother told us, "to be strong." But towards the end, when Jesse was like an old man, always limp in my mother's lap and harmless to anyone anymore, as I lay sleepless in the top bunk listening to him moan in his sleep almost every night, across the cramped room we three boys had to share in that green-shuttered rental house the last three months Jesse was alive, I prayed for him to die. By then, Jesse always had at least one black eye, and bruises everywhere—on the tips of his fingers and thumbs from all the blood tests, in the crooks of his bone-thin arms and the backs of his hands and the insides of his wrists from all the transfusions, on his elbows and knees and shins from even the slightest bump or fall. His stomach was distended from his swollen liver and spleen, the lymph nodes behind his ears so swollen that he always had a finger in his ear from the constant throbbing, and the glands at his jaws as swollen as JFK's had been when he'd been shot that same month Jesse fell into his first coma, that same awful November in Dallas. By then, the last two months, the only way my parents could keep Jesse from bleeding to death was to take turns every other day driving to Wadley Clinic to give a pint of their whole blood in the mornings, and then to return in the afternoons, haggard, exhausted, to get their own blood back, all their platelets spun out for Jesse. By then, all I could see anymore when I knelt in the pew every morning before class, and looked up at the crucified Christ over the altar—his head fallen limp and bleeding from his crown of thorns, his knees and elbows bloody from falling, his hands and feet pierced, his body gaunt, bloody, and gray—was my own brother hanging there on that cross. And all I could do anymore was pray to God to take him, soon, soon—not just to end his suffering, but to end my own.

Once, a month after Dr. Speigal's diagnosis of leukemia and Jesse's return from his first long stay at Baylor Hospital, my father brought home a punching bag, a bowling pin-shaped blow-up clown with a sandbag base that caused the clown to pop back up, grinning, every time Jesse punched him hard in the face, and Jesse and my sister Emma both fell laughing to the floor. Ever since they'd heard his diagnosis, my parents had been bringing home extravagant gifts for Jesse: a bright stripe-billed Toucan Sam and a stuffed panda bear as big as Jesse, a red metal tractor for Jesse to push up and down the driveway like a tricycle. Whatever he saw, whatever he wanted, he got, but he destroyed everything almost as soon as he got it—chewing off the toucan's plastic beak; ripping a hole in the panda's face and tearing out handfuls of stuffing, then scattering them all over the house; ramming his tractor into the hallway wall, over and over again, until the tractor's steering wheel fell off and there was a huge knee-high hole in the Sheetrock. The punching clown, my father told my mother, might help the kid let off a little steam, without hurting his brothers, his sisters, or himself.

But like all his other gifts—the Tonto outfit and the bow-and-arrow set from the Jaycee's, the Superman costume from my mother's sister Netta, the motorized police car from my mother's parents, Hanny and Pop Pop—Jesse soon grew bored with the clown, always more interested in hitting Nate or me instead, knowing we couldn't hit him back; always more interested in getting his hands on the toys Nate and I managed to get, one way or the other. They were ours, after all, not his.

One Saturday afternoon, when Nate bought a green Luger water pistol with the dollar Hanny had given him at the QuikStop down at the corner of Beacon and Columbia, where Pop Pop's old service station used to be, Jesse threw down his new police car, the wheels flying off, the electric motor shrieking to a stop, and he grabbed for the pistol. Nate gave it to him without hesitation, without a word, sweet kid that he was, and stood there squeezing his eyes shut while Jesse squirted him over and over again in the face. His shirt was water-soaked by the time Hanny walked into the room and stopped Jesse, took the water pistol away from him for a while. I wouldn't stop him, though, wouldn't take anything from him anymore. By then, I wouldn't even go near him most of the time, except when he'd fallen or hurt himself, whenever there was any threat from harm. I'd become one of his fiercest protectors by then, along with Emma and my father, no matter what he'd done to Nate, or to me.

The same thing happened a few days later with the rubber dart gun Pop Pop bought Nate to replace his lost water pistol. Right off, the moment he saw it in Nate's hand, Jesse dropped the water pistol to the floor and never looked at it again. And, right off, the moment Nate saw that Jesse wanted it, he handed the dart gun over to him, then each of the darts, one at a time. "It's okay, son," my father told Nate. "Let him have it. We'll just get you another one, okay?" But my father never did get Nate another one, and Nate never said a thing about it one way or the other, never said much, anyway, except when he talked to GI Joe in our bedroom closet. He just picked up the water pistol Jesse had taken from him at the beginning and walked out smiling to the front porch to play.

The dart gun was with Jesse for months after that and during his next long stay at Baylor, when he'd just learned new words to make my parents flinch—*tee tee* and *doo doo*—from the encephalitic boy with the frog eyes and basketball head who shared his room and died the next week. When Jesse saw Pop Pop the week after that, walking through the hospital room door, he said, "Butt!" and shot Pop Pop from the hospital bed, the rubber dart sticking between Pop Pop's eyes and staying there because Jesse and Emma'd both spit on it. The two of them laughed so hard they both peed Jesse's hospital bed.

Emma was always climbing into bed with Jesse whenever Hanny and Pop Pop took us to visit him at Baylor, was always climbing into bed with him at home, tickling him and laughing with him and sleeping with him, reading to him when my parents were too tired, always too tired. She read him *The Cat in the Hat* or *Miranda the Panda Is on the Verandah* until he'd memorized every line, then brought his red portable record player to his bed, endlessly playing tinny, scratched 45-RPM kids' records, or stealing my parents' 33-RPM records from their RCA console downstairs. Then they'd both recite together the story of Niki Niki Timbo Oso Rimbo Uma Muchi Gama Gama Guchi, the Japanese boy with the longest name in the world, so fat that he got wedged into the well. Or they'd laugh at Soupy Sales or Bill Cosby or Jonathan Winters records. Or they'd sing along with *West Side Story*, or *South Pacific*, or the Beatles's "Hard Day's Night," while I played Ringo's drum parts on my knees with my cardboard coat-hanger drumsticks. Or sometimes late at night they sang a nonsense song they'd made up together in Jesse's bed—almost a hum, a whisper, a secret song that only the two of them could understand:

Hi gee gee, ho wee wee,
No boddee oddee oddees hum num nuh.
No meeto, no dreenko, no munnee have aye nun ...

When Jesse was back at Baylor again, he'd save Emma the strawberry Jell-O or lime sherbet from his bland hospital dinner tray, even though it was mostly melted by the time we all came to visit from Hanny and Pop Pop's, because Emma liked sherbet and Jell-O, and the cold sometimes hurt Jesse's gums. Sometimes he'd let her play with the electric switches next to his bed, would let her move the bed and its stainless-steel guardrails up and down, then let her pet his pricked and bruised arms, taped to the transfusion boards, when he'd let no one else except the nurses touch him there, not even my mother sometimes. Emma wiggled the plastic tubes coming down from the clear plasma bottles and red transfusion bags and laughed, pretending the tubes were worms or snakes, then kissed the crook in Jesse's arm or his wrist or the back of his hand over and over again, where the white tape was, where the needles went into his veins.

One Sunday morning after Mass at St. James's, we all sat in the waiting room at Baylor, Hanny checking her watch for children's visiting hours to begin. We all heard Jesse's high, shrilling scream from the end of the ward, and Emma jumped from Hanny's lap, running like a big loping cat down the long corridors to Jesse's room. When she saw my mother holding Jesse down while the attending nurse tried to find a vein that hadn't collapsed, and stuck Jesse's wrist with the needle again and again, Emma turned over the nurse's cart, then the transfusion tree next to Jesse's bed, and the bottle hanging from it shattered to the floor. Then Emma picked up Jesse's dart gun from the nightstand, stripped off the rubber suction cups, and started shooting at the nurse's face.

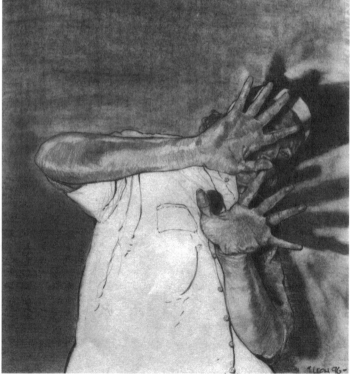

My father ran around the bed to catch Emma and she ducked, throwing the dart gun at him, then took off her black Sunday shoes and threw them as hard as she could at the nurse. My father chased Emma around the bed as she tiptoed through the splinters of glass that slit into her toes through her white cotton socks. Then she slid and fell into the pink slick of platelets and glass and blood plasma. When my father'd finally caught her up in his arms, Emma kicked him and hit him and spit in his face and bit him and shouted, "Stop it, stop it, stop it!" He draped Emma, kicking, over his shoulder and carried her back out to the waiting room, held her by her wrist high in the air, and paddled her backside hard with his open hand as she swung there.

"What in hell's wrong with you, little girl?" he shouted. "You want to tell me that? Do you? Do you?"

Then Hanny shouted, "Travis!" and my father handed Emma over to her, walked straight past the nurse's desk, and pushed the elevator button down, spending the next two hours pacing and chain-smoking in the hospital parking lot.

Emma didn't cry once during her whipping, didn't even cry when the head nurse peeled off her sticky wet socks and tweezed the glass slivers from her bare feet, swabbing the dots of blood sweating from her heels with rubbing alcohol. Emma just sat in Hanny's lap in a waiting-room chair, panting, her blue eyes fierce and pale, like the snow leopard's we'd seen at the Marsalis Zoo in Oak Cliff the summer before Jesse got sick.

After that day, Jesse threw away the rubber suction cups from the darts and started taking aim at my eyes when I walked into his room at Baylor, at the eyes of the new hemophiliac boy in the bed next to his, and my father finally had to take the dart gun away from him for good.

Jesse hardly ever touched Emma's things, or my other sister Hanna's. Emma brought his miniature piano to his bed all the time and let him hammer on all the keys till most of them had gone dead or fallen off, and she let him scribble loops all over her Crayola drawings of bright birds and mermaids on her bedroom walls. And all it took from Hanna was one of her brown-eyed, dark looks when Jesse walked in on Ken and Barbie's wedding, or approached Hanna's Kenner Kitchen with its light-bulb oven and cardboard refrigerator, and Jesse knew to stay away. But even more than Nate's things—his plastic pistols and GI Joes and Tonka trucks—Jesse wanted mine: my Paladin wallet cards (*Have Gun, Will Travel*), which he took from my dresser drawer one morning and played with in his bubble bath till they'd shredded apart, or my round-levered plastic rifle from *The Rifleman*, which he broke in half against the mimosa tree in our backyard, or my gray, felt Confederate cap from *The Rebel*, which he threw up on the roof of our house while I wasn't looking. My father found the cap months later when we were moving out, sun bleached and mildew rotten in the rain gutter. More than these, though, Jesse wanted my plastic models, the kits from Revell and Lindbergh and Aurora I'd glued together and painted, and bought with money I'd earned from mowing Hanny and Pop Pop's lawn in east Dallas: my X-15 and Mercury Redstone rockets, my Spitfire and Corsair warplanes, my Red Baron's triplane and the Spirit of St. Louis, and especially my monster kits, the Frankenstein Monster and the Werewolf, Dracula and the Mummy, and the Creature from the Black Lagoon.

Before Jesse was sick, I'd kept my models on my dresser, or on the shelves my father had built into the wall of the bedroom which I had all to myself in our new house. But three months after Jesse fell ill, when he was big enough to stand on the end of my bed and pull them all down, he began playing with them while I was away at school. When I caught him and told him he couldn't play with them anymore and took them away, he waited until I was gone and threw them all against my bedroom wall. I glued the models back together as well as I could, and my father helped me hang them from the ceiling with the thread my mother used to sew patches onto the knees of my jeans.

"Travis," my father said, standing on one of his barstools, looping white thread around the end of a thumbtack in the ceiling, "you got to understand, son. He's not even three yet. He's just a baby, you know?"

That year, for my tenth birthday, my father bought me a balsa model kit—a Sopwith Camel like the biplane his father had once co-piloted at Fort McNair with an RAF pilot during World War I, while chief engineer for the sanitary-sewer division of the U.S. Army Air Corps in Washington, D.C.

Two weeks before my birthday would have been my grandfather's seventieth birthday. When my father'd gone out to the grave site at Restland to clip around his father's granite headstone and cut fresh bluebonnets from the roadside for the bronze vase, he remembered the summer before his father died in 1945, when Truman bombed Hiroshima and Nagasaki and ended the war. My father'd stayed in a dormitory with his father at Texas A & M University, while his father designed and built an X-ray machine he used to analyze paving-asphalt aggregates for the Texas Highway Department. And, my father told me, he remembered his father buying plans for a Sopwith Camel balsa kit on his tenth birthday that summer. The two of them traced and cut the balsa stock for the cowling and other plane parts from the plan's paper templates, then into strips of ribbing for the fuselage and wings, laying white tissue paper over the ribbing and gluing it there, wetting the paper and watching it dry and stretch taut, then painting it with clear dope and camouflage paint and taking it out and flying it only once for thirty minutes one afternoon at Kyle Field, where the Texas Aggies played their football games.

It was the only summer my father'd ever spent much time with his father alone, he told me while we worked, the only thing they'd ever really done together, just the two of them. My father wished later that he'd paid more attention, because he didn't know it would be the last time, had no way of knowing that the X-rays would bloom the black mole on his father's shoulder into a melanoma, and that his father would die the next summer at the house in Houston which he'd bought for his mother and spinster sisters.

It took my father and I four Saturdays to build the Sopwith Camel, time he spared for me when he didn't have time—not with his new partnership, Hazard and Phelan Associates, Architects, not after his partner Hap had lost the big high-rise job he'd said would make them both rich and raise enough money to fly Jesse to the Mayo Clinic. Jesse watched my father and me work together at the kitchen table, shuffling in his pajama feet across the Mexican tiles, standing on his toes and picking up the half-finished tail rudder, saying, "Daddy, can I have it?"

My father took it from him and said, "No, Jesse boy. Sorry, but this one's for your big brother." Then my father looked at me, at the worry in my eyes, shook his head, and said, "My God, Travis, do you have any idea how much you're like my father? So damn *serious* all the time. Cheer up, will you, for crying out loud?" He put me back to work, sanding the plane's tail rudder while he hooked the long rubber band into the propeller's eye hook, then fed it back through the hole in the fuselage to the eye hook in the tail.

"You paying attention?" he said a while later and laughed, then shook his head.

That last Saturday, just as we'd finished dipping the red and yellow target decals into a bowl of water and slid them, slick, onto the Sopwith Camel's camouflaged wings, Jesse came shuffling into the kitchen, crying, his pajama tops bloody, a snotty drool of blood stringing down into his palms, cupped under his face.

"Daddy?" he said.

My father squeezed his eyes shut and said, "God, oh God," then shouted, "Helen!"

We didn't fly the balsa biplane for another month after that, weeks after my tenth birthday party at Hanny and Pop Pop's, which my parents had missed because Jesse was in ICU vomiting blood for three days straight. When my parents brought him back home, he was still terribly sick—swollen neck and stomach, stick arms and legs, like a poster child for CARE or UNICEF, except for his white skin, his straight blond hair, and his fierce blue eyes, like the pilot lights on the gas stove—and he was still in danger of hemorrhaging again at any time. It had been Jesse's longest stay in the hospital up till then, and my father'd made him stay in his bed all the time, wouldn't let him go anywhere in the house with all its high, angular balconies and stairs and tiled steps between split levels, wouldn't let him go outside either, not even when I'd bothered my father so many times after he'd gotten home late from work that he finally agreed to take me out to fly the Sopwith Camel in the cul-de-sac down the street.

"Why don't you let him go outside with you?" my mother asked my father that Saturday afternoon, as he stood winding up the propeller with me at the front door, one eye closed against the smoke of the Lucky Strike between his teeth. Jesse held onto my mother's pant leg in the foyer, crying, a bruised thumb in his mouth, his chewed and frayed Tony the Tiger bath sponge wedged between the tip of his nose and the crook of his forefinger. "He just wants to watch you fly the airplane, honey. That's all. He thinks you're punishing him."

My father stopped winding the propeller and nodded over to the big bay window facing the front yard from the dining room. "He can watch us fly the damn thing from in here."

"What's it going to hurt for him to go outside, Travis, you want to tell me that? You're being unreasonable."

"No, Helen."

"I'll go outside with him, then, all right? I'll make sure nothing happens. Will that make you feel better?"

"Goddammit, Helen, I said no."

"It's a beautiful day out there, Travis, and it's not going to hurt him to get a little sun. He could use a little sun, you know that."

"No," my father said. "*No.*" He huffed out a sigh and a puff of smoke, then shook his head and nodded over at me. "Jesus, Travis," he told me, "get the front door, will you?" He stepped outside and looked back at my mother, her arms folded, Jesse crying behind her leg in the doorway. "I don't need this from you, Helen," my father said. "This is the last goddamn thing I need from you right now, you know?" Then he turned and kicked the front door shut behind him.

In the circle down the street at the dead end of Broken Bow Road, my father said, "All right, son, all you got to do is hold the propeller like this and hold the fuselage here, back by the tail. Then just let the propeller go as you toss it off. Like this." My father snapped his wrist twice without letting the plane or the propeller go, then said, "Get it?"

"Got it."

"Good." My father handed the plane over to me, the propeller slipping from my fingers and spinning out in my hands. Then my father shook his head and said, "Jesus, Jesus, Travis. All right, all right, just wind the damn thing back up again, will you?" He took a long drag from his Lucky, closed his eyes, and tilted his face up into the afternoon sun, sighing smoke up at the sky.

I held the plane up to let it go and glanced over at Jesse in our house down the street, sucking his thumb, his forehead pressed up against the bay window. Then I looked back at my father.

He folded his arms and said, "Go on."

"What if it crashes?" I said.

"It won't. Not if you keep the nose up. Just keep the nose up, all right?"

"I can't," I said. "It'll crash."

"If it crashes, it crashes. Worse goddamn things have happened in this world."

I held onto the propeller, held the plane's nose up, held my breath. I looked out at the street ahead of me, at all the houses, the parked cars, the telephone poles, the wires strung taut between them.

"I don't want to," I said. "I changed my mind."

"Give me that goddamn thing," my father said, and snatched the plane away from me. Then with one quick pivot of his forearm he sent the Sopwith Camel into the air, gliding only about fifteen yards before landing on all its rubber wheels with its nose up, bouncing over a dip in the asphalt, then turning and bumping to a stop at the curb.

"See?" my father said. "It didn't crash. I told you it wouldn't." Then he walked to the plane, stooped to pick it up, and handed it to me. "That's enough," he said. "I've had enough. Enough. We'll fly it again some other time." He walked back to the house without waiting for me, without even looking back.

In my bedroom ten minutes later, I laid the plane on my bed for just a moment, to go to the bathroom down the hall, and when I came back Jesse was standing there next to my bed in his Superman suit, the Sopwith Camel smashed at his feet. Feeling a fist rise in my throat, I fell on him, held him down to the floor, and hit him in the stomach, then in the face, and Jesse started screaming and then Emma ran to my door and started screaming in the hallway, and my father pulled me off and threw me against my dresser, knocking a drawer out on top of me, clothes spilling everywhere.

"Oh God," my father said, falling to his knees next to Jesse, and pulling Jesse's pajama tops up around his stomach to check for the blue spread of a hemorrhaging bruise. He cupped Jesse's face in his hands, turning it left and right, then opened his nostrils and peeled back his lips, to check for bleeding gums.

When he saw that Jesse was all right for the moment, my father turned to me, red faced, a single blue vein under the skin at the thinning red hair of his widow's peak. Then he fell on me, pinned me to the floor, and pressed his forearm hard into my windpipe till I choked. "Don't you ever hit him again, ever,

ever," my father shouted, hitting me once hard in the stomach, then hitting my thigh and my ribs with his fists, again and again.

"Travis!" my mother shouted from the doorway, and fell on my father's back, pulling him off me.

My father stood, wild-eyed, looking at his hands as if they belonged to someone else, then looked down at me, took in a breath, and said, "My God, Travis, do you understand what you could've just done? Do you have any idea? Well, let me tell you. You could've killed him. He could've died. Do you understand me? Do you?"

"Yes, sir," I said, holding my stomach, thinking at any moment I'd throw up. "I'm sorry, but he did it on purpose."

"I don't care. I don't give a good goddamn what he did. I don't care if he burned the whole goddamn house down. Hell, they're going to take it away from us anyway. Don't you ever do that again, do you hear me? *Ever.* We can replace the goddamn house. We can replace the stupid goddamn *plane.* But we can't replace him, do you understand me? Do you understand what I'm saying?"

"Yes, sir," I said. "Yes."

My father pressed his palms into his eyes a moment, pulling his fingers down his face. He turned to my mother, who knelt next to Jesse, checking him just as my father had done moments before. "Do you think we should take him to Baylor, Helen? What if there's internal bleeding? I just don't think we should take any goddamn chances here."

"He's all right," my mother said. "I think he's all right."

"I'm taking him to Baylor right now," my father said. "Go get his overnight bag, and I'll call the hospital to let them know we're on our way."

"No, Travis," my mother said, stooping to pick up Jesse, hitching him up to her hip. "Let's wait. I'll call Dr. Speigal first, to see what she says. Then I'll watch him. I'll watch him close."

"We'll both watch him," my father said. "Tonight we'll watch him in shifts."

"You can't afford to lose any more sleep, Travis, you know that," my mother told my father. "And what about your big meeting with Zimmerman tomorrow?"

My father sighed. "Hap'll just have to handle things tomorrow."

"You can't afford to have Hap handle things tomorrow," my mother said.

My father stepped toward my mother, then stopped, his blue eyes half-lidded, fierce, and pale. "You always contradict me, Helen, do you know that? Do you just *have* to contradict me every goddamn minute of every goddamn day? Look, I don't need you arguing with me right now, telling me how to run my goddamn business, all right?"

My mother blinked, her head cocked, her mouth open a little, as if she'd just been slapped. She shifted Jesse from her hip to her shoulder.

"Go put Jesse down on the couch," my father told her, "and watch him till I call Dr. Speigal, all right? Do you think you can do that?"

My mother looked down, nodded, and followed my father out of the room. As she passed through the open doorway, Jesse looked down at me from over my mother's shoulder, his face changed, his eyes more afraid than I'd ever seen them. I was afraid, too, and sorry, more than I'd ever been. When my father turned back in the doorway and looked at me sitting at the end of my bed, his face was changed, too, the face of a man I'd never seen before, his eyes a cold blue, burning, like Pop Pop's white German shepherd Hey-Boy's, after he'd eaten all the pups in the litter and Pop Pop had to shoot him with his .22. My father swept his hand across the room, pointing to my underwear and T-shirts and rolled socks scattered all over the floor, then to the twisted balsa wood-and-tissue biplane we'd built together. "This room is a mess, Travis," he said. "Clean up this goddamn mess, will you?" Then he kicked my bedroom door shut behind him.

Neither of my parents could sleep that night, and neither could I. And though it turned out that Jesse would have only a shiner the next week—his left eye swollen shut the next day, a blue half-moon turning to black and then to yellow—I was sure he'd die that night if I slept. I stayed awake all night and prayed that he wouldn't die, half hoping that he would, then hating myself for that hope, hating myself for being sleepy and then for not being able to sleep, for closing my eyes and then for not being able to close them. I lay staring up at my patched-together warplanes above me, ready to dive and fall, staring up at Dracula and the Werewolf and the Creature from the Black Lagoon dangling from the white threads hanging from my bedroom ceiling, their mouths and hands black with blood in the dark.

By then all of us were becoming insomniacs. Jesse turned and moaned in his bed across the room we shared in that green-shuttered rental house on Estate Lane, which we'd moved into a month later, and I held my pillow over my head half the night, then got up and padded down the cold linoleum tile of the hallway to my parents' room, and said, "Mom, Dad, he won't stop." Then one of them, my father, my mother, got up, exhausted, and followed me back down the hallway to our bedroom and picked Jesse up, his pillows and sheets covered with sweat and sometimes blood, and took him down the hallway to their room to toss and moan in their bed between them, pressing his hot, sweaty face into my mother's face all night, his thin, bruised arm slung out over her neck.

Other nights my mother rocked Jesse in the dark living room till dawn, creaking the red Naugahyde rocker with cigarette burns on its arms. Or my father walked half the night through the dark house, wearing his dress slacks with no shirt, his dress shoes with no socks, smoking one Lucky after another, the bright ash wagging in the dark hallways, the ice tinkling the sweating glass in his hand, as he paced the hall past our bedrooms. Some nights my father left us gifts for the morning, like the one I found on my dresser, as I packed the last of the boxes to move out of my room on Broken Bow: a Guillows balsa model kit of a German BF-109 Messerschmidt, with a note taped to the box, saying, "I couldn't find another Sopwith Camel, son. I looked everywhere. I'm sorry." Then some nights my father just came into the room we three boys shared on Estate Lane and stood over Jesse's bed, just stood there for hours sometimes, till I whispered from the top bunk, "Dad?" and he left the room without answering, without saying a word.

Other nights Hanna sneaked into the kitchen and ate the entire layer of chocolate from the Neapolitan ice cream in the freezer, or all the Hershey's semi-sweet morsels my mother had hidden in the pantry for chocolate-chip cookies. Or Nate got up in his frayed and yellow-stained skivvies, and closed the door to our closet, clicking it shut, then whispering to GI Joe half the night. Or sometimes he just lay awake in the bunk beneath mine, kicking the slats holding up my mattress, keeping me up half the night, snoring like a man, grinding his teeth in his sleep till I thought they'd break off in his mouth, rolling around in his bed, kicking off his sheets and blankets, and mumbling, "No, no," till I'd throw everything on my bed—my sheets, my blankets, my pillow, my bedspread—to cover and muffle him again. And even then I couldn't sleep.

And then, some nights, when everything was quiet and I was finally dropping off, Emma'd come to our bedroom doorway, wide-eyed, listening for Jesse's breathing, and when she knew he was there asleep in his bed, and not in my parents', or in some hospital bed all the way on the other side of Dallas, she climbed into his bed and spooned up to him and hummed to him half the night their secret song in the dark.

GEORGE CLARK
Writer

Interview

by Linda Burmeister Davies

The subject matter of George Clark's fiction varies widely. In the past two years, we've published "Seven Stories for All the Animals," an emotional piece about an ex-soldier and his beloved animals; "Two Seasons on the Continent," which convinces us that one

George Clark

man's narrative paves another man's road; and "Backmilk," a tense, tender story about a hungry newborn who dares betray his ancestry.

Clark is of British and Xhosa descent and was raised in Rhodesia and South Africa, where his family passed for white. Drafted into the South African Defense Force, he spent two years as a reconnaissance platoon leader in Angola, and later enlisted in the U.S. Army Infantry to earn money for graduate school. Sandwiched somewhere between the two, he toured Europe and the Americas as a Celtic musician with The Kinsmen.

*Clark now has his Ph.D. in English and teaches creative writing and multicultural literature at Florida State. His short stories have appeared widely; his first collection, **The Small***

Bees' Honey, *is forthcoming from* **White Pine Press** *this fall;* *and his first novel,* **Harmony Church,** *is well underway.*

Together with his wife Rikki (whom he met in Germany, where they were both in the U.S. Army), their new baby Rorrie, older daughter Courtney, and a substantial family of animals, they live—for now—in Florida. Next destination? Perhaps the Northwest, or maybe the Czech Republic for a few years.

DAVIES: You mentioned a few minutes ago that it was easy to look down on other people's tastes, easy to suggest that someone should be reading somehow "better" material.

CLARK: Yes. For instance, I think if a kid is reading Stephen King, they're reading, doing better than 99% of the rest of the world. It's like when people make fun of other people's musical taste, and I think, *They're listening to music, they're enjoying themselves, do they have to listen to experimental jazz fusion?* I fall into it myself; it's so easy. One of the things my students have to do is what we call portrait papers, where they interview someone outside of their world. It can be the person who cleans their dorm, or somebody they walk by everyday but would not think to talk to. The students are very resistant at first, but it becomes their favorite paper. They can write it up anyway they like— from the first-person point of view, or a third-person point of view where they are just one of the characters. I encourage them to talk to the friends of the interviewee and to describe the surroundings. They really enjoy it. And they're wonderful papers for me to grade. I ofttimes will get details for characters from things that I see or that my students see.

Oh, for your own writing.

Sure, sure. I'll just go, *Wow, this is a really great detail, can I use that?* and they'll say, *Oh, sure.* They love it. And I always do the things that I assign my students. When they have to do an adventure paper, something they've never done before, I'll do something as well. For example, karaoke. I'm deathly shy in front of crowds. I thought it would be a good thing to get over and so I sang "Like a Virgin." It was a lot of fun.

Did you get over your shyness?

Not at all. It's like parachuting—I thought that would help me get over my fear of heights, but it didn't. I did get over my claustrophobia by caving in north Florida. You get into these narrow little rooms and sometimes you get wedged, and your partner will have to pull you out by your feet. I think I've pretty much beat the claustrophobia for the most part. I wonder how much is in our background and how much is learned. I think the fears that are learned you usually beat, like insects, for example. That was a learned fear of mine, and I have no problem with it now. I had a revulsion toward flies after Angola, where I fancied that the flies that got caught up in my food had feasted on the corpses from my platoon. I don't have that anymore. Well, not as much. I used to keep flyswatters and spray in every room. Then I realized that was silly. When you live with someone you can see what your obsessions are a little easier. Rikki was very understanding, but I was a bit embarrassed. But the adventure papers are really fun for me because there are all sorts of things I've wanted to do. I even learned to rollerblade, and I'd never before rollerskated. Where I grew up, that was only for girls.

How did you decide to get your doctorate, and what did you do to accomplish it?

It's odd. I think I drifted into it, pretty much how I've sort of drifted through most of my life. I'd gone into the American army so I could get college money, but I was thinking I'd just get a second bachelor's and I'd get it in English since I'd already been working as a journalist in the army. So I took an English course as a special student. It just happened to open up. I did very well in the class—I loved it. It was just sort of luck or ... it seemed like the perfect thing for me. It was what they call a piggyback course with graduates and undergraduates, and I asked my professor, David Kirby, *What's the difference between what I do as an undergraduate and what graduates do?* He just grabbed me by the arm and took me into the department and got me into the graduate program. Then I took a creative-writing class just wanting to know what *they* did, and I did terribly. My stories were unreadable, fluffy, and light. But after that, I was hooked.

I think Rikki [George's wife] was right when she said that when a person is really involved in a story, the story gains substance and strength.

Yes. At first I did not want to write about anything in my life.

I was really struck when you said earlier that your father, in a drunk, revealed his background to your mother, that she "looked at him and looked at me standing in the doorway, and, before breakfast, she was gone." How would you describe your growing up?

I would say just a standard childhood; by standard, I guess I mean repressed, Victorian. An exacting father who wasn't around all that much, and a mother who left somewhat early when she found out that my father was one-quarter black and that we were all one-eighth black. But I think that there are a lot of people who have had worse childhoods. I mean there was a lot of good stuff. It was a great place for me to grow up. Once my mother left, I was basically unsupervised. I could stay out all night. I could do anything, really, that I wanted to at that point. It could be tough, but there were things I could do that most kids don't get a chance to do.

And how old were you?

Around eight.

How old were you when you decided to go for your doctorate?

I'm thirty-nine now, so I think I was about thirty-two when I got out of the army, and even after I got my master's, I never thought I would get a Ph.D.

But you did. It's impressive.

It is and it isn't. I was impressed with myself in the sense that nobody in my family has really gotten much education. Every once in a while somebody will take a college course now, but there are also people that never finished high school and even made fun of people that went to college. So I felt proud in that way. But then, when you actually get your Ph.D., it is a sort of letdown because you realize you're not …

Not transformed?

Yes. I thought I'd be this eggheaded intellectual and also that I'd be a lot wiser, and of course I'm not. I still do really bone-headed things all the time. I'm insensitive and stupid. There are times when I do stupid things and afterwards ask myself, *What was I thinking?* It can be a bit of a letdown, but then there's also a plus. I could get hit by a bus now and I'd still be *Doctor* Vegetable, you know? They can't take that away from me. Ultimately, I think nobody really cares. Or a few people might. If somebody knows that you have it, they might be afraid to talk to you because they feel that you'll be thinking, *What a stupid thing to say*, if they say the wrong thing.

I have to admit I've always been intimidated by big degrees, thinking how much those people must know that I don't.

I saw lots of parallels between getting my Ph.D. and getting through the army. If you do everything they tell you to do, you'll get through it. Even at the end, they give you this green form that you have to take around to the Dean of Arts and Sciences, the cashier, the English department, and they stamp things and initial them. I don't think it takes so much intelligence as perseverance and the ability to follow instructions. As they say in the army, "Pay attention to detail." I think more people could do it if they really wanted to. It's really just not that important for some people. I needed something that I could stick with and that would get me back to a regular person again.

Again?

From when I was living at home, I guess, when I was still in Rhodesia. After that I never stayed anyplace very long.

Why is that?

Well, I don't know. I got my bachelor's degree in the States, and got married in South Africa and had a family, but when I lost my wife and my son—they were killed at home when I was in the army—I just couldn't stay in one spot for a long time. When I got out of the South African army, I would keep coming back to the States to spend time with my daughter, and then I'd go to South America or Europe to live for a while, and then come back.

I didn't know. I knew you had a family earlier, I just assumed the usual loss by divorce.

Oh no. Everybody's got sad stories. My wife has had to deal with much more than I can ever really even think of dealing with. She was abused as a child and I can't imagine that. I might have been a bit neglected, but that's about all. It's a bit arrogant for somebody to say, *My pain is worse than your pain.* I'm very happy with Rikki and with our daughter, and our dogs and our cats, and where we're living right now and what I'm doing, the classes I'm teaching. I like what I'm writing. But all of that can be taken away. If you lose the things that make you happy, what is left? If there's nothing left, people commit suicide or become homeless. You have to make sure that there's something of yourself in your life outside of your family, or your job, or anything like that. You should be able to lose it all and still have a person left.

Did you lose your wife and child because of the wars going on in that region?

No, no. It was disconnected. A crime. And unfortunately, my daughter, who was unharmed—she was just a baby, but I think babies know things—for a long time she was very, very quiet. You never know what they know or what they can sense—we rely so much on our eyes and our memory. Much more information is passed on by our sense of smell than by our eyes, and yet that's one of the most neglected senses.

Your stories cover such a wide range of emotional experiences. I know that you have gathered many of those experiences from your own life, but I wonder how easily you take in other people's stories or imagine them when you look at them. Do you feel like you empathize easily with other people?

When I work at it, I can be empathetic, but generally I am very self-centered. It's something I have to work at. My stories usually are a combination of my experiences and the experiences of other people. The novel I'm working on is bizarre and darkly comic, and yet almost everything in it either really did happen or nearly happened, or is an exaggeration of something that happened. Yesterday I saw a pair of very expensive sunglasses in the bottom of a urinal and started thinking of what the story was behind that. Did they belong to a very fastidious person that would never touch them again? And then, of course, nobody else would. There are so many stories going on right now. I've been thinking, and we've spoken a bit, about what sort of properties stories might have if we could find some way to investigate them. For a long time we had no real concept of time, and now we have it measured and logged down, and yet it's affected by gravity, it's affected by the rotation of the earth. Time is different on Jupiter than it would be here, but we run our entire lives by it, and it strikes me that we run our lives by stories as well. For example, when we dream, we want to explain our dream. Dreams are pretty nonsensical when we first wake up, and yet the more we tell them, the more they start to fall into a story. I think we organize almost everything into stories. Stephen Hawking said he suspected if we broke down the universe, we would have time and energy. I wonder if maybe those are just a couple of the pieces. Perhaps dream and story might be two more. Why do we dream? That's a complete mystery to me. That dreams and story are outside of time is also amazing—you can fall asleep for a few minutes and have an entire dream crammed into those few minutes, seconds really, and time will stand still. It's the same with a story: you can read a book, an entire book that covers one day of time, or you can read something like *A Hundred Years of Solitude*, and it might take you a good weekend to get through a century of story time. You can close it anytime and pick it up again, and when you do, you're back in the time of the book. That's where [my story] "Two Seasons on the Continent" came from. There's so much coincidence in our lives, and coincidences could be going on all the time that we just don't recognize. What are the ramifications of a story? How many times have people been driven to do things? You ask people, *Why did you do that?* and they say, *I don't know what got into me.* That's happened to me. I'll do something completely irrational. When I was writing that story, I thought what if somebody were telling a story and that somehow affected me?

What a thought! Sometimes we really do have to wonder about our paths: How did we get here? What is this unexpected moment? We work so hard for so much, and yet some of the most significant things that ever happen to us have nothing to do with our efforts.

Yes. And so much of what we work so hard for is completely meaningless. It's easy to get caught up with things. I've been struck by the obsession, in this country, with happiness. The idea of happiness as a goal is completely foreign to me. I mean it's nice, but it's like saying I only want a part of life and not the whole of life.

So what goals did you grow up with?

Work hard, it doesn't matter if you like your job, it doesn't matter if you're satisfied, you just work hard to provide for your family, look to take care of yourself in your old age, and then die.

What would you choose now?

Mine are small goals. I guess I have some larger goals that are starting to take shape. There was the Ph.D. goal, and I want to learn German. I have all the mechanics down, but I would like to learn German fluently. I'm trying to learn to play the concertina.

You play a lot of instruments. It looks like you played the concertina when you were with The Kinsmen.

Yes, I did play some songs on the concertina, but they were just songs I learned from practice. You could probably teach a monkey to play the concertina like I do.

I don't know the instrument.

It's a squeeze box. It can be a very melancholy instrument and also I've heard it played where it really lifts your spirits. I would like to be able to put some of myself into playing the concertina instead of just playing the notes. You have to have something to do, some sort of goal in front of you, but it doesn't really matter what it is, it doesn't at all. Yesterday, at the Seattle Bumbershoot festival, I saw this guy playing a fiddle on a large unicycle and I thought, *That's as good an accomplishment as any I can think of.* What difference would it make even if you became the greatest writer of this century? You would be forgotten in a few centuries. What's the difference if you're forgotten in a few centuries or if the year after your book comes out, it's on the two-dollar shelf of Books-a-Million?

Would you finish the sentence for me please: Most people are basically _____.

Oh. I think most people basically want to do the right thing, but we lose sight of it. I don't think there's any person who sits around and says, *I'd like to have a war,* or, *I would like to set up a large business so that I can treat my employees terribly,* or, *I would like to foul the environment to make a buck.* I also don't think there's anybody in control, that there are a few people running everything for pure profit and power. It's very easy to get sidetracked. Instead of happiness, our goal should simply be to *do*—I don't want to say what we were *meant* to do, but perhaps what we *ought* to do without anyone telling us what that is. That's what's so distressing about the religious right. They're trying to legislate away our free choice; people should be allowed to make the wrong choices, people should be allowed to mess up. That's part of being a human being—only by making terrible choices can we discover what the right choices are.

Rather than being obedient, which is a different thing altogether.

Yes! Having poured through the New Testament a number of times—it just goes to show how everyone reads it a different way—it seems to be about being nonjudgmental and allowing other people to have freedom of choice. Those are cornerstones of the Gospels. I tried to find a church I could go to, but now I get a sense of revulsion when I enter a church. I just cannot make myself. I'm sure there are good churches out there. I'm wondering if I'm just not meant to be a churchgoer. I went to so many. I went to one where they spoke in tongues.

Did that scare you?

Yes! I thought they were just doing it to impress each other—before I went. But if they weren't really speaking in tongues, they certainly believed they were. It's odd how paranoid you can get, because they were perfectly nice people, but it was frightening. I didn't know whether they were going to turn on me and rip me apart and eat me. You just don't know what to expect. And yet you have to respect their spiritualism. They were deeply spiritual people and I felt a bit sheepish after I left, and I thought, *They weren't going to do anything to me.*

What languages do you have knowledge of?

I have lots of bits of languages. I know the swear words and the food in dozens and dozens of languages.

Dozens and dozens?!

Well, no, I shouldn't say that. The Romance languages: I mean, oftentimes you can speak Spanish in Italy and you can get a good set of directions and perhaps figure out the menu. I know some Xhosa, and a *patois* they speak in the South African Defense Force which is a mixture of Bantu words and English and Afrikaans. I know some Afrikaans, and English, of course. I also know some German, but I really want to learn a language the right way, using proper grammar. I don't want to speak like a four or five year old. There are so many bits and pieces of language in my stories, but that's all you get because that's all I've got. I grew up in a very chauvinistic, English-is-the-right-language way. I would get in trouble for speaking Xhosa, even sayings which would find their way into everyday life. Afrikaans was not spoken widely in Rhodesia because that's a South African language, but there were lots of South Africans in Rhodesia, so certain words would come out in slang. I wasn't allowed to use them at all. It was considered an inferior language. I remember my mother would not let us use glottal stops.

Wow. Forbidden sounds.

Yes. My father grew up in London—my family left South Africa before moving back to Rhodesia—so he had the cockney accent where you kill the middle consonants of a lot of words. I wasn't allowed to do that. Contractions were somewhat suspect as well. We were supposed to speak proper English, really no other languages. It bothers me now because in later life, it becomes much more difficult to learn a language. That's why I'm studying German. I'd like to move back to Germany for at least a few years, but it really doesn't matter if I use the language. It doesn't matter if I ever use my Ph.D., which I very well may not. I'm not exactly sure how I'll be received on the job market.

What do you mean?

I'm wondering, if you don't fall into an easy category, exactly what they'd do with you. The fact that I spent so much time in the military. It could mean absolutely nothing to them.

So you have an ongoing consciousness of your identity and its suitability.

It could be just with me. But I guess I'm suspicious on that account. It would be wrong for me to bill myself as an African American. It would be one thing if I hadn't passed for white in one country to take advantage of the system, but then to pass for black in this country for any advantages I might get—it would be wrong. Although I think our whole family got what they deserved for passing for white. It caused nothing but grief. It would have been much better to have just been honest.

Why?

Well, because when it came out, it obviously caused problems between my mother and my father, and us as well. I doubt if I would have been in Angola. There are all sorts of things that you think are benefits but they're really not. And then I think about growing up under a cloud of secrecy.

Many of our readers are writers. Writers often start with autobiographical materials that they are pushed internally to write. Do you have recommendations for people to help them create a piece of fiction that works?

One thing is to try not to embellish too much. I mean, you can add things from other people's experience that relate. I like to throw everything into a story. Someone tells me there's too much going on in a story, I'll throw in more stuff, because life is complicated and I think a story should be as well. There are so many things that are acting upon us. If you want a simple motivation-action sort of story then you should go into the juvenile-literature section. Life is not that simple. But at the same time they should trust their experiences. I ofttimes have my students write down the strangest job or the worst job they've ever had, or whatever seems to stand out in their minds. One person used to clean out chicken cages, which to me would be the most awful job in the world—the stench, and I'm not a vegetarian, but what a cruel existence. I had a professor who used to repossess wigs. If they didn't make their payments, he would go and get their wigs. I had to wear the Winnie-the-Pooh costume [an upcoming story talks about this]. I was claustrophobic and my head was stuck in a honey jar like in the story. You should just trust the material. That's where I get in trouble. After I first write a story, I spend all the drafts trying to take myself out of it. I mean as a writer, taking out clever little sentences that don't belong or forced humor or forced pathos. Though I don't think you ever really succeed. Then you have the story in its purest form. But our egos get in there and we want to be responsible for the writing, we want to show our hand all the way through the story. It's difficult to take yourself out and say, *Okay, I'm going to take this really pretty piece of prose that I've worked on for an entire week, and kill it.* If it doesn't fit, it will jump out at the reader. Also, where a story ends is where it ends—I've written on for four and five pages before I realize where the story really ends. It's difficult to delete those pages. That's why when I make changes to a story, I don't want the old versions of the story to be around, I don't want to see them, so when my computer says, *Replace file?* I always do.

That takes courage.

I think that's a strength of my writing. My stories are very pedestrian in their initial drafts. I have to take things out and not try to direct the reader as to how they should feel about what's going on in the story, but rather just let them see what's going on, hopefully give them all the elements, if I'm doing my job right, so they can understand the story and get something out of it. If they get something completely different than what I've intended, that's okay as well, but I think there should be something for the reader to do.

Does language play much of a role in our dreams, in your opinion?

Yes. I have a niece who speaks in Afrikaans in her sleep because her mother is South African and she grew up with both languages. But she doesn't realize that she's doing it or remember how to speak that language except when she dreams. I wonder how much exactly language plays in dreams. My dreams are more images and situations that shift from one to another. Sometimes I'm a character, sometimes I turn into somebody else. There's no rhyme or reason. I try to be honest when I recount them afterwards, and they make absolutely no sense that I can see. I look at them in the morning as long as I can remember them, and then they disappear as the day wears on. Rikki's will stay, but they get more ornate with each telling. I'll hear her tell a dream that she's already told me and it will start to make more and more sense. That's something that Freud talks about in *The Interpretation of Dreams*, that we want to order our dreams. But I don't think it's necessary. Any benefit we get from the dream, we receive when it takes place. So many people are obsessed with writing them down, keeping dream notebooks and things—I don't know if it makes any difference other than that it's interesting.

Susan and I spend a lot of time talking about our dreams over lunchtime and we think we figure things out. It's a great medium for us to work out things about our lives.

I often think, *Why did I dream this particular dream?* and if I think long and hard enough I can find some parallel situation. I wonder if it's our brain sort of warm-booting itself, or if there's some other reality that's going on. It's difficult to know. The entire thing is odd—having your creativity on one side of your brain and, on the other side, the means to communicate it. How do you translate?

It all has to go through our corpus callosum or whatever that's called. I wonder if that's really our soul through which everything passes. Don't they sometimes disconnect it for medical reasons?

I always thought of it as a wall; I never thought of it as a soul. If this were your soul … remember that guy who had a rail spike driven through his head? I think this was at the turn of the century—it's in all the beginning psychology books—I think they were blasting a tunnel or something, and this spike went right through his head, and after that he turned mean. He could no longer complete a task without swearing at someone, his wife divorced him, his friends left him. For a while he traveled in a freak show. But if it were his soul—it's funny, I hear things like that and I wonder could I write a story about that? What if your soul was in between there and it was driven out and you were a soulless man? Last night there was a television show we were watching while we were getting the baby into bed, and it was a documentary on emergency medical technicians, and they spoke about a "golden hour," when a person would live or wouldn't live as they're trying to get them through the emergency. I thought that would be a wonderful time for a story to take place.

We've published several of your stories and in preparation for this interview I read some of your newest ones. There were three that I literally had to stop and cry over; it was too hard. That included "The Pit-Bull Drill"—

Really?

Fleming was just too much for me. I agonized over that guy.

After I wrote "The Pit-Bull Drill," I felt I developed as a writer, and so I rewrote it into the novel as the voice of the squad. In the novel, there's not a first person, but rather a limited-omniscient narrator that jumps from character to character with a gesture or a look, a glance. I stole it from Flaubert in *Madame Bovary*. They pass the narrative baton on to another person, and then there's also a first-person plural which is the collective consciousness. I stole that from Conrad in *The Nigger of the "Narcissus."* I'm really excited about getting a chance to write on the novel again. I wanted to do something to break the myth of boot camp as a positive bonding experience. Instead of having characters who bond together and go off and fight two dimensional enemy soldiers in a foreign war, I wanted to have them fall upon themselves in basic training. I interrupted you: you said there was another story that disturbed you. "The Pit-Bull Drill" and ...?

"The Pit-Bull Drill," "Astral Navigation," and "Politics of Rain." Was there really an Uncle Blas? Were these stories his, yours, or did they come from other sources?

I meant, as grim as it was, for there to be some humor in Blas's story, in the way he told it, the offhanded way—it jars. That's how the novel will be. Uncle Blas came from a photograph of a black butcher, which I thought was a fitting occupation, who had fought in the Bay of Pigs. There were lots of Cubans in Angola who were fifty years old, unlike the American Army, where most retire after twenty years. I wanted a soldier who had fought at the Bay of Pigs and in Angola. In the photograph, he had this enormous goat belly, one of those tight bellies, where if you hit it, it would hurt your hand, but the rest of him was very fit, and he was jet black with a huge cigar and a beret. He's barechested, wearing dark blue dungarees and combat boots, and I thought, *He's perfect!* I can't just make up a character. Some people can, but I can't. There has to be some element, something I've read or seen. I do a lot of research, even on things I've experienced firsthand.

Your experience is extremely varied.

That's why it's almost going to be comical when I go on a job hunt. I'm wondering if they're going to think I'm going to goosestep in a beret and uniform.

You don't give that impression at all.

I don't want to be confused with my narrators, but they are all a part of me in a sense. In the novel there are thirteen people in the squad. I think that each one of them is a different aspect of myself, which is why I think the collective-conscious voice fits so well. None of them are very attractive characters, but hopefully the reader will sympathize with them.

If you'll let me go back to Fleming for a moment, he was an extremely vulnerable guy: tall, weak, trusting, and unable to protect himself for whatever reason. He eventually went off and lost his mind. Have you ever felt like you were pushing your edge?

I'd be surprised if everyone hasn't at some time or another. There were a couple of years where I basically holed up in an apartment and watched videos and read books and spent time with my daughter. I had different apartments: when the season was off, I moved closer to the ocean and later I'd move away— just furnished rooms as close to the ocean as I could get. I'd move about every six weeks and everything I owned fit in my car: a suitcase of clothes, my great uncle's war chest, a statue that I got from the Dominican Republic, and a painting from Haiti. I'd put the statue out and the painting up and I was home. I didn't have a kitchen because I never cooked. That was a very low point in my life. Other than my daughter, I didn't interact with anybody. There was also—and I didn't even know I did this until I met Rikki—a tendency when I was stressed to fall quickly into a deep dream where I couldn't be woken until it was over. I haven't done that in a long time. I think that happens to all people sometimes where they shut down. Maybe a good counselor can help people to shorten that period. Most people will heal themselves. Like with Rikki, for example: being abused as a child is so difficult, to the point where your mind is not really able to function for a while. For a long time she was on psychotropic drugs to control her depression. It took years and years for her to heal, but she finally did.

And she probably has gained a great deal of perspective after going through it all.

We have to get through these things. There's a certain perverse part of my nature that finds the hard way, at least for me, is always better. That's why I'm trying to get rid of the television, get rid of the car, as much as possible—I don't want to be a fanatic about it. Like last night, that taxi was wonderful. I like mass transportation, but when you have a lot of groceries to bring home, it's nice to have a car.

I definitely take the easy road sometimes. I admire the simpler route.

It's funny, I was thinking about that when you were talking about how farm animals are treated. I agree one hundred percent and yet I still eat meat. It's almost like a culture, like beer is a culture in Switzerland, Germany, and Austria.

You have quite a few animals, don't you?

Yes. I had more. "Seven Stories for All the Animals" is one reason why I wonder if stories aren't outside of time. Much of what happened in that story was a rehearsal for what was going to happen and ultimately did happen. That was a terrible thing. The person that owned the next-door neighbor's house kept pit bulls in the backyard, and he only fed them two or three times a week. One dug under the fence and killed the goat. It was just gore all over our porch and everything. It was a terrible way for him to go. Fortunately, livestock tends to go into shock at times like that. We were also dogsitting for a collie at the time, and she ran out of the yard as soon as we opened the gate. I had just helped somebody move furniture all day, and now I'm running after the collie for two or three miles in my big clunky boots, knowing that the goat was still waiting to be buried. It was one of the most awful days of my life because it was never-ending. When I caught the dog it panicked and bit my hand, and I wasn't going to let it go, but it bit through my glove. So then I've got a rag wrapped around my hand, and I'm up to my chest digging a grave, and all sorts of thoughts go through my mind, and memories.

What a painful day.

It's funny, but I felt as awful that day as I felt any day in Angola, and I realized that it was just as important as what was happening then.

When we published "Backmilk," you provided a wonderful picture of your great grandmother. What gifts do you imagine she would, or has, bestowed upon your children?

It's odd, but it's sort of like a guardian angel looking over us. There's a great deal of ancestor worship in a lot of African cultures, and I wonder if some of that hasn't rubbed off on me, because I feel very aware of my great grandmother, and yet I know almost nothing about her. Much of what I write is filling in gaps of stuff I couldn't possibly know. That's how I came to write "Backmilk." It's a merging of my life and my daughter's life, because I couldn't really tell you what happened in my own infancy. But I can see my daughter's birth, so I merge the events together, and I wonder how much of all this comes from my great grandmother. It does seem to blur a bit. I would like to think that I am getting an idea of the importance of spirituality. It seems so hokey, so corny to us when we're younger, and there's also the if-you-can't-explain-something-it-doesn't-exist idea that so much of our culture has. If you see something out of the corner of your eye, you say, *Oh, it was nothing.* We take our dogs to the cemetery all the time and if they skirt a particular grave or they stare at something, I wonder, *What are they looking at? Oh, it's nothing.* In Africa, I knew somebody who actually ordered a different file cabinet because he believed that all matter has a spiritual nature, and that this particular file cabinet had an evil nature because he sometimes could not find files in there. I've thought about this because I've had to file, and I've looked and looked for a particular file and said, *It's not in here.* Then somebody else has come right to where it should be and pulled it out. I can't explain things like that. Or my car is running out of fuel, it's been on empty for a while, and I talk to it and say, *Go further, go on,* when it's sputtering. I talk to it, beat on it, curse it, encourage it. I think there are all sorts of ways we believe these things but we don't let ourselves admit it. We don't let ourselves admit that anything exists that we can't explain or that isn't tangible and concrete.

We do try to say those things aren't there, but I don't think we'd have to say it if we didn't think they were.

If you look, you'll find that the vast majority of the world believes in some sort of afterlife. They believe in ghosts. They believe in the spiritual nature of matter. So we're really in the minority. We look down at them and it's easy to tut and say, *Oh, these primitives.* Yet I wonder what they might think of us. They might think we're obstinate and blind.

I've always believed in ghosts. I grew up with that idea from my mother. But I've never thought of things having a spiritual nature. That's a new idea for me.

Ah, but it's a very old idea, and of course not the same as meaning that this cup of coffee is listening to our conversation. They don't believe that. Things don't translate very well between languages, and so a ghost or a spirit or many of these terms sound different in our language, and they have different connotations than they might in Xhosa. My undergraduate degree is in political science and economics, and there were African students who would ofttimes bring up spirits when they meant … I guess the sixties term would be "bad karma," "bad vibes."

What about that file cabinet? Did he think the file cabinet itself had a way about it, or rather that some other spiritual nature resided there, or what?

Not the file cabinet itself, but something that resided there. Perhaps the cabinet had belonged to a person who died. You have all kinds of ancestors, you see. There are ancestors of legend who founded the village in which they are worshipped; there are ancestors who died long ago, outside the memory of the living; and then there are the recently dead.

How would someone who truly knew you and loved you describe you?

I don't think anybody truly knows me. Rikki's probably come close. Answering this would require that I think an awful lot about myself, something I try to avoid. It's not that I hate myself or anything. I just don't feel comfortable examining myself and saying I'm this sort of person or that sort of person. I think there came a time in my life when I realized exactly what kind of person I was and what I'm capable of doing. That's not necessarily a bad thing, but I don't have a lot of illusions about being a nice person, a person that could say, *Oh no, I could never do that*, or, *I could never do this.* I think every one is capable of anything. I don't think that a person is necessarily who they say they are, but rather how they behave. I've heard some people say they're very laid back and casual, and they're anything but. It's so odd. Or you meet somebody at a party and they've had some traumatic event and they say, *But I'm over it now*, and you think, *But this is the first thing you told me about yourself. Why are you telling me this?* If anyone truly knew someone, there'd be maybe two reactions, total love and total revulsion. I'm more interested in what I can do and what I'm supposed to do rather than worrying about things that I've done, or the type of person I might be.

Pete Fromm

As a kid, I never liked this picture much, the embarrassing failure of my ungrown teeth to close on anything. But it still hangs in my parents' home, and I'm getting used to it.

"Dry Rain" is the title story of Pete Fromm's newest collection, due out in May from Lyons & Burford. His other books include the story collections *The Tall Uncut*, and *King of the Mountain*, the novel *Monkey Tag*, and the autobiographical *Indian Creek Chronicles*, winner of the Pacific Northwest Booksellers 1994 Book Award. He lives in Great Falls, Montana.

PETE FROMM
Dry Rain

ith one hand clamped on Joey's forehead, Stil shouts into the phone, "What? What?" He locks his elbow, keeping Joey a full arm's length away.

Joey yells, "Just let me talk to her! I'll tell her it's okay!"

"*What?*" Stil bellows into the ancient phone, a rotary dial for Christ's sake, like Canada was some third-world country.

"I'm okay, Mom!" Joey shouts. "We're having fun."

Slashing the phone to his side, the booth rattling as the cable hits its limit, Stil hisses to Joey, "Would you? For one second?"

Joey quits shouting and Stil wraps his hand around the top of his son's head, hauling him into the booth, a finger on one ear, a thumb on the other. He presses Joey's face against his side, then carefully lifts the phone back to his ear. "Now, Tracy," he says, shouting again, "you were saying what?"

Stil listens.

"You *do* owe me!" he roars. "I had a life with you! You owe me for that!"

Suddenly Stil pulls the phone away from his ear, stares at it, clamps it back to his head. Dead. Hung up. He stares at it again, then slams it against the box on the wall.

The phone breaks neatly in half and Stil stops, already halfway out of the booth, having always pictured himself hanging up on her just that way, but thinking it was impossible; phones are made of something from NASA or someplace, something that could tolerate reentry, splashdown.

When he looks down, Joey's head is no longer pinched beneath his hand. Joey's out in the street, holding the black earpiece of the phone, shouting into it, "What? What? *What?*"

Stil smiles shakily. "Get out of the street," he says, though he guesses you'd have a better chance getting hit by lighting than a car in this speck of town.

Hopping onto the sidewalk, Joey wallops the booth with his piece of phone. "What?" he yells.

Stil fingers the change in his pocket, still American coins, and not many of them, two bucks maybe. This is all taking longer than he'd supposed.

The day's blazing, and Stil pulls his shirt away from his skin. Beyond the single street, the few stores, and the post office, they're surrounded by nothing but fields. Thunderheads loom tall in the hazy sun, rain smearing from their bottoms, maybe reaching the tabletop of land, but probably sizzling out before getting the chance.

"Virga," Joey says.

Stil looks at him. "What?"

"Virga," Joey says. "That's what it's called. When the rain can't reach the ground."

Stil glances from his son to the clouds and back. "It's just dry rain," he says. "Depressing as hell."

Joey looks a second longer. "I like it," he says.

Then, turning away from the sky, Joey taps the phone on his thigh. "What did Mom say?" he asks.

Stil watches the rain going nowhere. "How would I know?" he answers. "Couldn't hear a word with your howling. Could've been a wrong number for all I heard."

"What'd she say?" Joey says again.

Stil stares down at his boy. He rattles the change in his pocket. Two bucks, he thinks. "Is there something you haven't told me?" he says at last. "Something about your ears?"

"I hear everything," Joey answers.

A shiver wracks Stil's shoulders. He pulls his hand out of his pocket. "Let's get something to eat. What do you figure they eat up here, anyway?"

"Grass," Joey says.

Stil smiles. The whole place does smell like cut grass, some gigantic golf course, wheat or hay or whatever they grow.

"Can people eat grass?" he asks.

"If they're hungry enough," Joey answers. He looks at his phone and yells, "What?" into it. "*Mom?*"

"Knock it off," Stil says.

In the cafe Stil stares at his change. Two dollars and forty-four cents. There are a few damp bills in his wallet.

"We're rich," he says to Joey.

Tracy has all the money in the world. Stil knows that. All she has to do is share. Stil wonders if she has a warrant out, if the border guys will nab him as soon as they see Joey yelling "What?" into his chunk of phone.

They're the only people in the cafe and it's a while before a waitress peeks out from the back. Stil whispers, "Put that thing away," and Joey hides the phone beneath the table.

"American money?" Stil asks as the waitress approaches.

"This is America, too," she answers.

"U.S."

She looks at them. "Sure," she says. "Straight across."

A thirty-percent hit on the exchange. "Can't keep this up long," he says to Joey.

Joey shrugs. He bangs the phone on the bottom of the table and the waitress jumps.

"*What?*" Joey yells.

Stil shakes his head. "It's been kind of a big day for him," he explains. He orders a hamburger.

The waitress tilts her head toward Joey.

"We'll split it," Stil says, and the waitress edges away.

"You want to get us arrested?" Stil whispers to Joey.

Joey opens his mouth to shout "What?" but Stil stops him.

"Take it easy," Stil says. "Mom might've misunderstood all this. She might've called the cops. We got to play it cool."

"But …"

"But quit acting like a loon," Stil interrupts.

Joey lifts his phone to his ear, whispers, "Now, you were saying what?"

Stil shakes his head. "A parrot," he says. "A fucking mynah bird." He apologizes for swearing.

Joey shrugs.

"We'll call again after lunch," Stil says. "Find a phone that wasn't personally installed by Alexander Graham Bell."

The waitress sets the burger in the center of the table and scurries away. Only one plate.

"How much are you trying to get for me?" Joey asks.

Stil takes time cutting the burger in two. He lifts the bigger side in his hand. "It's not like that," he says, shaking a big loop of ketchup onto the meat. "I told you before."

"You get me out of school," Joey recites. "We cross into Canada. You call Mom. You call her three times. You never call Mom."

Stil, with his mouth full, says, "Eat your burger."

"I like cheese."

Stil rolls his eyes and calls for the waitress. "He wants cheese on his," he explains.

"On just the half?"

Stil shrugs. "He's on vacation."

The waitress whisks up the plate.

"Melted," Joey says, shaking half a phone at her.

Stil gives him a little smile and the waitress retreats.

"This is like gangsters," Joey says. "Mom'd kill me."

"Just take it easy," Stil answers. "Before the Mounties surround us."

Joey laughs.

"What's so funny?" Stil says, setting the last bite of his burger down on the bare table and wiping his mouth. "Could happen."

The waitress returns Joey's half and he studies the melted cheese. "What're we going to do next?" he asks.

"We got to call again."

"About the money," Joey says. It's not a question. He stuffs the last of his cheeseburger into his mouth. "We should rob a bank."

Stil can barely understand him around his mouthful. He eyes his boy as he chews, remembering how sharp he is. He wonders where in the world that came from. Not from him, that's for sure. Not from his mother. Some kind of freak of nature.

"So, you like living in the Big Sky?" Stil asks, trying not to remember sitting slumped in his car watching the huge house, the grassy cuts of the ski runs behind it, the lawyer and his kids coming and going, and Tracy—Joey's whole new family.

"It's okay," Joey answers. "Not as bad as you think."

"What makes you think I think it's bad?"

"You hate lawyers," Joey says.

Stil rolls his eyes, but Joey keeps pressing. "We're in Canada, Dad. We're making ransom calls."

"Now, goddamn it, Joey, I did not kidnap you." Stil tries to keep it down, but he's shouting a whisper. "I told you that. You're my kid. We're supposed to do things like this. It's good for you."

"You didn't even get visitation, Dad."

"Only lawyers worry about that crap."

"Lawyers and cops."

"Same thing," Stil answers, looking out at the blistering street. He remembers playing with tar bubbles in the road on days like this and he asks Joey if he ever does that.

"What kind of bubbles?" Joey asks.

"Never mind," Stil says. He stands up, checks his wallet for the last of the bills—fewer of those than he'd hoped, too.

"Let's go."

"To call Mom?"

Stil asks the waitress where he could find a pay phone. She holds out his change, pointing vaguely down the block. Stil wonders if she's already called the Mounties, if they really wear those goofy red uniforms. When Stil dials this time, Joey is quiet, waiting just outside the booth. While the phone rings, he pokes his head in long enough to say, "A hundred thousand. At least."

Stil reaches to push him out, and as his hand clamps around his head, his soft, thin hair, Joey squawks, "Well, I'm worth it, right?"

"You're not kidnapped," Stil says. "Jesus …"

"Then take me home," Joey dares.

"We're on vacation," Stil hisses. "That's all."

Tracy interrupts then, her voice fuzzy, but just as daring as Joey's when she says, "Vacation my ass. You want to know what the FBI thinks of that theory?"

"Tracy," Stil says.

"You're talking to them right now," she says. "Every call's being recorded. What in the world are you doing in Canada?"

Stil's shirt has long since been soaked through in the heat, but now it's different, the smell of fear changing everything. Canada could be a guess. Last time, she hung up on him. She wouldn't do that if the FBI were tracing the calls. But Stil knows Tracy can do anything, FBI or no.

"I just want what's coming to me, Trace."

"Coming to you! For what? Child support?"

Stil thinks. "Vacations aren't cheap," he says.

He listens to her deep, tired sigh. "You're broke, aren't you?"

"We don't have enough to come home," Stil admits. He can't stand how good it is to hear her.

He hears another voice in the background, a deep rumble.

The FBI, or just the lawyer, getting impatient.

"Trace," Stil says, "you didn't really call the cops? The FBI?"

"Bring him back, Stil," Tracy answers. "Think of him, would you?"

Stil glances at Joey, standing outside the scratched glass, his piece of phone clamped to his ear, straining to hear.

And, as if he does hear every word, Joey suddenly yells, "We're having fun, Mom! I am!"

"He's enjoying it," Stil whispers.

"For God's sake, Stil."

"He is. You should see him."

"That's exactly what I want."

"Me too," Stil says, even more quietly.

"Bring him back and this is over, Stil. All forgotten. But I swear to God, if you ever touch him again …"

"I had a life," Stil says, cutting her off. He has to look away from Joey. "It's eye-for-an-eye time now, Trace." This time he hangs up on her, letting her chew on that until he finds another phone.

He steps out of the booth, waving for Joey to follow. "We got to hit the bricks, kid," he says.

"Is she tracing the calls? Are they closing in?"

When haven't they been, Stil thinks. But he says, "Vacation, Joey. They don't trace calls for a vacation."

Joey stops, looking close at Stil. "My school is for gifted, Dad," he says. "Not gimpy."

"I know, Joey." Stil opens the car door and waits for Joey to scoot across. "You just don't know anything about this."

"Then tell me."

"I don't know anything about it either," Stil answers.

Joey buckles his belt. He lifts his phone to his ear, then switches it to his mouth, whispering, "I had a life."

"Don't you ever say that," Stil snaps. "Not ever." He yanks at the key and they pull onto the road, heading west, back toward the mountains, the beautiful lives beneath the ski hill. He's paralleling the border, staying as close as he can.

She has to cave at the next call, Stil thinks. He glances at the map on the seat, deciding they'll cross over at Chief Mountain, drive through the park like a real vacation. Joey'll be home in time for Tracy to tuck him in.

She couldn't have called the FBI.

Stil glances at Joey. He's finally let go of the phone. It sits on the map between them, the broken end sharp and pointed like a quick, homemade weapon: a jagged beer bottle held at your throat. "Think of him," she'd said.

Stil rubs at his temples.

As the road climbs they leave the wheat country and its dry storms behind. The air blowing through the windows cools slightly. "It's nice up here," Stil says, his voice scratchy. They haven't spoken in a long time. He clears his throat. "Smells good."

"Pine trees," Joey answers, staring out the window.

"Conifers. Pine, spruce, fir, hemlock, cedar."

"Smells like one of those deodorizers." Joey grins.

Stil makes himself smile. "How do you like that? Living in a place that smells like a giant Christmas tree hanging off your dash?"

Joey keeps smiling. After a while he asks, "Where do you live now, Dad?"

"I got a place," Stil says, so fast it sounds like a lie even to him. "Not far from where we all lived."

"In the desert?"

"On the edge."

"Never smells like this?"

Stil looks at his wrist crooked over the steering wheel. "No," he says.

They drive miles more and Stil asks, "You ever miss Arizona?"

"Mom calls it Bedrock. Like the Flintstones."

Stil nods. "Bedrock," he whispers. Their whole lives turned into a cartoon. He pushes his wind-blasted hair back flat on his head and pulls onto the shoulder, the smell of the pines everywhere.

Joey looks at him, wondering, and, looking away from his eyes, Stil sees that Joey's shoes have pictures of Batman on the sides.

What the hell would Batman do now? Stil wonders. Probably *Kapow!* the hell out of him and fly Joey back to his mother.

"You like Batman?" he whispers.

Joey shrugs. "He's okay."

"When I was a kid it was Superman. He was everybody's favorite."

"He died," Joey says.

Stil can't look at the little shoes. He glances out the cracked side window. "Are you ten yet?" he asks.

Joey looks down at his bare knees. He moves the point of the phone in tiny circles against his skin. "Almost," he says.

"What do you think we should do?" Stil asks.

Joey puts the phone to his ear. "I can't hear you."

Stil says it again.

"What do you mean?" Joey asks.

"I mean right now. Jesus, I'm driving around Canada with a genius and I'm trying to figure everything out myself."

"I'm not smart about everything," Joey says with an apologetic shrug.

"You like that school?"

Joey scrunches his face. "School?" he asks.

A motorhome lumbers by, real vacationers. "Man, we used to have some knockdowns about that," Stil says. "Me and your mom. I just wanted to let you be a kid, you know. But she was 'accelerated this, accelerated that.'"

Joey picks at a tear in the seat vinyl.

"You remember the first day you came home from the special classes? Goddamn, you couldn't've been six years old. You told us you quit. You said, 'It's supposed to be accelerated, not excessive.'"

Stil laughs. "I about busted a gut, but Mom got you all turned around. Marched you right back the next day."

"It wasn't that bad," Joey whispers.

"Well, you're definitely the thinker here, pal. What should we do?"

"Mom won't give you any money for me?" Joey says, his voice so small Stil has to lean close to hear.

"Joey," Stil starts, but then takes a big breath. "I need the money," he admits. "I'm busted flat.

"But that's not why I got you," he goes on. "I did that just to show her. Just to show her what she did to me."

Joey picks up the phone. He holds the unbroken half to his mouth. "Did you even try to keep me? Get visitation?" He flips the phone around, the good half to his ear now, waiting.

Stil shifts behind the wheel. He puts his hand on the stick, his foot on the gas. But then he slumps low, the same position he'd watched Joey's new house from, watched him walk out to school alone, the lawyer's kids older.

"Not then," Stil says. "I couldn't right then."

Joey nods, the phone clamped to his ear.

"I wanted to," Stil begins fast, but Joey turns the phone around to speak into it.

Stil stops to hear him whisper, "I had a life with you. You owe me for that."

Stil glances quickly out the window. He begins to say, "Don't say that," but instead drops the car into drive and creeps back onto the pavement. They drive along, Joey whispering into the phone, words Stil can't and doesn't want to hear.

"You want to go to Arizona with me?" he asks at last.

Joey looks up. Into the phone he says, "We'd starve, Dad."

Stil tries to smile. "We could eat grass."

"There's no grass in Arizona."

"On the golf courses."

"We'd never get memberships."

Stil looks down the highway. "I suppose not," he says. "Not to eat the grass."

Joey doesn't play along, and, taking a big breath, Stil asks, "You want me to take you back to your mom's house?"

Joey shrugs. "It's where I live now," he whispers. He looks out the side window away from Stil. Raising his voice just loud enough, he says, "I'll make her give you some money."

"Aah," Stil says, lifting his hand to wave off the offer, but he doesn't say anything else. He needs the money.

Stil drives faster than he should, especially if she's got a warrant out for him. He stops at one more phone, making Joey stay in the car while he talks to Tracy. When he gets back in, Joey wants to know what they said, but Stil doesn't say a word. He drives even faster, trying to make the roar of wind so loud he won't be able to hear Joey asking again and again about what they'd said, what they'd decided about him.

Not until the sign says they're approaching the border does Stil slow to a crawl. As soon as he sees the tidy, white custom buildings he pulls over, then backs up, out of sight. Immediately he wishes he hadn't done that, imagining nothing looking more suspicious.

He shuts the car off, to hear better if anyone comes at him. Then he turns to Joey. "Really," he starts, "Joey. I wasn't kidnapping you. I just wanted to show her."

Joey nods. "Just to show her," he says into the phone.

Stil closes his eyes for an instant. "That's not what I mean," he starts.

But Joey lowers the phone from his ear, not listening. He begins widening the rip in the vinyl, digging into it with the hard point of the broken end of the phone.

"I'm not going back with you, Joey. I can't cross the border right here."

"It's a vacation, Dad. They don't alert the borders for a vacation."

"Yeah, well, maybe she misunderstood."

"Yeah," Joey answers. "Maybe she did."

Stil opens his door and Joey does the same. They meet in front of the car.

"Mom's on her way," Stil says. "She's going to pick you up here."

Joey peels a broken grasshopper off the grille. He pulls off a wing. "Is she bringing the money?"

Stil looks down at the top of his son's head. "No," he says. "I don't think so."

"I'll send you some. Do you have an address?"

"I'll write. Let you know."

Joey glances up. "You never write, Dad."

"Well, I will now."

"For the money."

"No. For you. So you can write back. Tell me about that rain. That vertigo."

"Dry rain, Dad. Vertigo's something totally different."

Stil nods, picturing the drops starting out like regular rain, but burning up, then just gone. "Maybe Mom will let you come down to see me sometime," he says.

"Mom?" Joey says. He laughs.

"I suppose not," Stil answers. He brushes back his hair, his hands empty and useless.

Stil glances down the quiet road. "You shouldn't have to wait too long. She should be here soon."

Joey nods. "Did she really call the police on us?"

"I don't know. She says she did."

"She might have," Joey says.

Stil shrugs.

"Well, you better go then. Before the Mounties get here."

"Yeah." Stil kneels on the edge of the road beside his son. He puts his arm quickly around Joey, though they've never done much touching.

As Joey leans into him, resting the top of his head against Stil's cheek, Stil notices the tar webbing the road, thick bands of patching filling the cracks.

"Watch this," he whispers into his son's ear, and letting Joey go, he reaches down, pressing his finger into a swelling blister of hot tar.

The tar bulges away from his touch and he presses another finger beside it. Finally the bubble is trapped between his fingers and a block of solid tar. It pops, a slow motion balloon, leaking and settling back to the ground.

"Cool," Joey whispers.

"Sometimes you can lift out whole pieces, like rope."

"What do you do with them?"

Stil can't remember. He sees himself running through the streets of Phoenix, a lifetime ago, carrying a thick rope of hot road tar like a trophy. "Chase people with it, I guess."

"Who would I chase?"

"Your friends," Stil says, but he sees Joey walking out of the gigantic house by himself, his books in a heavy pack on his back, his head down, maybe looking for cracks, careful where he puts his feet, not breaking his mother's back.

Joey presses the toe of his Batman shoe against another bubble. It pops immediately. "Mom'd kill me for playing in the street," he says.

"Yeah, well," Stil answers.

Joey looks at his collapsing tar pocket. "She might be here already," he says. "I better go."

He lifts his hand just enough to graze it along Stil's. With his other hand he lifts the phone to his mouth. He's starting away when he asks, "Will you come back for another vacation?"

"You bet," Stil says, thinking what an awful wager that'd make.

Joey's walking away then.

"Joey," Stil calls. "Maybe you could ... ," he starts, then falters. "Why don't you come to Arizona with me now? We could work something out with ..."

Joey interrupts, raising his voice so he doesn't have to turn around. "I'll learn how to play with the tar before you come back, Dad," he shouts. "I'll know how."

"You bet," Stil whispers, his air leaking out as Joey walks away. Then he remembers. "Virga!" he shouts. "That's what it's called, Joey!"

Joey still doesn't turn around, only nods, and Stil slides behind the wheel onto the sun-hot vinyl. The bug-smeared windshield glares and it's hard for him to watch Joey walking away, waving once more over his shoulder, still carrying his broken piece of phone.

Mary Gordon

I am about to perform at my dance recital. This is
something I dread, but I know I should look happy.

Mary Gordon, professor of English at Barnard College, is the author of *Final Payments*, *The Company of Women, Men, and Angels*, and *The Other Side*, and two collections of stories, *The Rest of Life* and *Temporary Shelter*. She has received the Lila Acheson Wallace-Reader's Digest Writer's Award and a Guggenheim Fellowship.

MARY GORDON

Conversations in Prosperity

It is the last day in September, cool and dry. My friend and I are sitting in the park, a few feet from the gardens, admiring the cosmos and the columbines, which we know we are incapable of growing for ourselves. We are quite different, physically: she's tall and thin and blond, and I am short and dark and fleshy. She's wearing khaki shorts, a sleeveless blue shirt, and a denim jacket. I'm wearing purple leggings and a red cotton sweater. I have my dog with me, a seven-year-old black Labrador.

An older woman, alone, a very nice woman in a gauzy flowered skirt, a silk jacket that zips in front, tan Rockport sneakers, stops to pet the dog. She talks about her own dog, long dead. A cocker spaniel. How she used to come to the park with her dog and her son in a stroller. How one time a man gave her dog the rest of his ice-cream cone. But grudgingly. "Take it if you want it so much," the man said to the dog.

"I wanted to say to the man, 'Well, at least be gracious about it,' but of course I didn't," the woman says to us. She wants to talk. I focus upon the hem of her skirt, hoping it will move, indicating she's ready to leave us. We don't want to talk to her, we want to talk to each other. We love each other and have too little time to sit and talk. So much, too much, in our lives. We position our bodies so the woman will understand that we don't want to talk, but in a way that, we hope, will indicate that it has to do with our affection for each other, not our rejection of her. She does go away. We feel a little bad, but not for long.

Then a young woman, with well-cut hair that falls like a black slash across her cheek, flowered Lycra running shorts, a bottle of water, steps up to pet the dog. She says, "You have the perfect dog. You're so lucky to have the perfect dog." If she looked different, if her hair were less well cut, if her shoes were dirty, we might interpret these words as madness, but we know they aren't mad. Only, perhaps, a sign of melancholy. It's easier not to talk to her than the older woman, since it seems more likely that the future for her will be bright.

She moves away from us, not happier for having seen us.

Although we are quite different physically, my friend and I share a concern for virtue. My friend, who is a Midwestern Protestant, carries in her heart a sentence a philosophy professor said to her once: "What have you done today to justify your existence?" And I, raised by Catholics who mixed a love of pleasure with a sense of endless duty, carry in my heart the words of Jesus: "Greater love than this no man hath, than that he lay down his life for his friends." We have talked about this to each other, and we understand that both these sentences take for granted that just living is not enough. Something great, something continually great must be done because this thing "life" is not to be taken for granted, consumed, like a marvelous meal or a day at the ocean. My friend has in fact devoted her life to serving the poor. She's a social worker; now she's working with children in Washington Heights. I have not put my lot with the poor, and my friend's saying that I am heroically committed to an ideal of language isn't, I know, enough for me. I have not laid down my life. But my friend, too, feels she hasn't done enough. Some days we are so sickened by the events of the world that we can't read the newspaper. Then we force ourselves to read it, on the phone, together. We hate our political opponents with a vengeance that there is no place for in the ideals of the liberal minded. It is always on our minds: we haven't done enough.

And so we can't quite brush away the two women who wanted to talk to us, to whom we refused to talk. We wish we could be other than we are. Or we wish we could be seen clearly for what we are really. Not, as everyone imagines, people who are endlessly sympathetic, endlessly dependable, but people who deeply resent invasions on our pleasure and our privacy. No one understands our hunger for solitude, or that we could quite easily and totally give ourselves over and became voluptuaries. When my friend had a short space between jobs she spent a day naked, eating the box of chocolates her co-workers had given her by way of farewell. She finished the whole box sitting on her couch watching the Simpson trial. She said no one would believe her if she told them. As no one understands when I describe the days spent with the phone off the hook eating Milano cookies and reading *People* magazine. They say my friend and I only do these things occasionally, that we need to do them because normally we are so productive and responsible. What they don't understand is that we would like to be doing those other things quite often. Maybe all the time. That we would if only we could believe that we could get away with it. If these were things of which it would be impossible for us to stand accused.

I may be speaking only about myself. I think that, much sooner than I, my friend would give up luxury and put her shoulder, as she always does, to the wheel.

I might not.

Both of us have things to do the next day that we don't want to do. A visit to the country. A friend who has lived in a foreign city for years and is back in town. Both of us say yes too much, because we *do* like people, we really do, but usually not as much as we first thought we would. Or when they're not around, we don't like them as much as when we were with them, and certainly, we don't look forward to seeing them again. And there are always too many people with whom it would be moderately pleasant to spend time. We are not the kind of people who have to speak to women in the park who seem approachable because of the kind eyes of their dog.

My friend says that when she saw the movie *Il Postino*, she knew she would do exactly what Pablo Neruda did. Have an intense, deeply felt friendship with the postman. Then, leaving the island, fail to write. Then come back for a visit to the island, but too late, after the postman was already dead.

We talk about the sickening sense that you have betrayed someone simpler, finer than yourself.

The truth that for a certain time, it was right to say you loved them.

Realizing too that while you never thought of them, your face was always in their heart, behind their eyes.

My friend says, "I've never been left."

I say, "I haven't been left since I was twenty."

As we say this, we are not proud. We understand that what is missing in us is the impulse to surrender. We speak of another friend of ours who has been left, again and again. Dramatically. Midnight scenes involving things thrown out of windows. Furniture removed when she's gone to work. She has been left, and left greatly. I think of her when she dances with a man. She puts her head back, exposing her throat, as if she were ready for the knife. When I see her do it, I envy her the beauty of the gesture. And I envy the man who is her partner. If I were a man I would fall at her knees. Or put a knife to her throat. Perhaps both. Perhaps both, simultaneously.

My friend and I agree that we are both too old now to be left dramatically. Or at all. We've chosen good men, accomplished men with a secret streak of passivity which we may be the only ones to see. These men make a still center around which we move, purposefully, anxiously, believing we are doing good.

I ask my friend if she thinks it's a good thing for a man to love someone like us.

Or for a son to have us as a mother.

She tells me her son once said, "The thing about you, Ma, is that emotionally, you're very low maintenance."

We realize that no one we can in good faith call a friend is one of the poor. We know only one person who doesn't have health insurance. One who won't get social security. We both worry about these people and hope that if they're in need we'll have the wherewithal to help. By wherewithal we mean both money and good will.

My friend tells me about a woman whom she works with who has three children, a husband out of work, a mother with Alzheimer's in a nursing home, an alcoholic father in another nursing home. My friend says, "I think that I should genuflect to her. But there's nothing I can do for her. Nothing at all."

No one we know well doesn't have some sort of household help. A cleaning woman.

I tell my friend that when I was young no one I knew had household help, and that in the years when no one I knew had household help, I was left by men, or boys, over and over.

I suggest that it would be too simple to say this has to do with age and money.

But I don't know how else to explain it.

I confide that my closest male friend, J., had a cancer scare this summer. The day before he left for a month-long holiday, his doctor phoned and said the minute he came back, he had to schedule a biopsy. He was about to get on a boat to sail around the Caribbean. He did get on the boat, he went sailing, and he told the friend he was sailing with about his cancer scare. But he didn't tell me, although I'm the person he usually confides in, because he knew I was trying to finish a book and he didn't want to distract me.

When he finally told me after the book was finished, and the biopsy had come back negative, I was grateful that he hadn't told me before. Then I was appalled. I say to my friend, "I often think I'm not really capable of love. Or capable of real love."

I repeat to her for the thousandth time the story about my daughter and I when we were in a riptide. I didn't try to save her. I saved myself. Someone else saved my daughter.

My friend (the friend with whom I'm having the conversation), tells me that I panicked, that it doesn't mean anything about my character. And that I wouldn't have felt like that about our other friend's not telling me about his cancer scare if I hadn't been finishing a book.

I don't believe her.

I know that one day it will be clear to everyone: I am incapable of love.

We stop for a cappuccino, and though we know it's over-priced, we don't for a minute consider not buying it. $2.75. Too much, but nothing, really, in our lives. On the tables there are bowls full of packets of sugar. I tell my friend that if I were one of the poor, I'd load my pockets with these packets of sugar; it would make a big difference. Perhaps I'd allow myself a coffee— not a cappuccino like this, but a plain coffee in a plain coffee shop—eight-five cents—once a month. Each time I did this, I'd fill my pockets with sugar. I'd have to choose a different coffee shop each time because if I were one of the poor, I'd be noticed.

But, my friend says, if we lived in a really poor country, there wouldn't be packets of sugar on the tables.

Because of the conversation we are having, we pick up the movie *The Story of Adele H.* from the video store. We can hardly bear to watch it. The daughter of a famous man, Victor Hugo, Adele puts herself in the place of the desperate. For love. For unrequited love. She condemns herself to wandering. To starvation. Beneath our pity and our fascination, there is gratitude. Because she has done it, we need not.

The next day, I copy a line from a book I'm reading, and mail it to my friend. It says, *Ready to be someone else in order to be loved, she would abandon herself to ridicule and even to madness.*

Under the words I write,

Adele H., but not us —

Today it is the fifth day of October. My friend meets me in front of my son's school. A little paradise, this school, where children can be happy as they learn. A private school, with a very high tuition. Leaning against the building is a woman wearing a white clown's wig, bell-bottomed jeans, a blue bra, and no shirt. I have neglected to mention that it's raining and she appears to be at least seventy. And that she's not wearing shoes.

My friend and I don't say anything about her.

No one entering or leaving the building appears to look at her.

It is not possible that anyone entering or leaving the building will speak to her.

It is also impossible to invent anything that might approximate her history.

My friend and I don't say anything about her because we both know she's the woman we're afraid of becoming.

The one we fear becoming when we have lost our prosperity.

The one we really are.

*Siobhan Dowd and Jake Kreilkamp—program director and coordinator,
respectively, of PEN American Center's Freedom-to-Write Committee—write
this column regularly, alerting readers to the plight of writers around the
world who deserve our awareness and our writing action.*

Writer Silenced: Win Tin
by Jake Kreilkamp

*B*urma is a country ruled by a military regime that goes
by the Orwellian name of the State Law and Order Restoration
Council (SLORC). It seized power in 1988, renamed the
country Myanmar, and killed between three thousand and

ten thousand civilians during pro-
democracy riots. In 1989, the SLORC
cracked down on Aung San Suu Kyi's
National League for Democracy (NLD)
party, placing her and many other
party leaders under house arrest, and,
in 1990, annulled elections that gave
control of the country to the NLD.
Even after releasing Suu Kyi in April
1995, the SLORC continued to wage
a public-relations war against her,

Win Tin

focusing on her reputed links with foreigners—in particular her
marriage to a Westerner, the Oxford University academic
Michael Aris. Security agents recorded license-plate numbers of

citizens who attended her weekly Sunday speeches outside her lakeside home. In recent months, dozens of members of Suu Kyi's NLD party have been arrested, and in the past month hundreds of people have been detained for attempting to attend one of Suu Kyi's speeches.

Suu Kyi's colleague, NLD secretary, editor, and writer Win Tin, is the only member of the original executive council of the NLD who is still imprisoned. While still a student, Win Tin began his career as a writer by working for the Burma Translation Society. After graduating, he went on to become editor of *Hanthawaddy*, one of Burma's major daily newspapers. Even before the SLORC came to power, Win Tin ran into trouble for his outspoken views of democracy and freedom of expression. In 1978, a paper critical of the Burmese Way of Socialism (the guiding program of the state at the time) was read at a "Saturday Reading Circle" of which Win Tin was a member. He was dismissed from his job, and *Hanthawaddy* was banned. Win Tin supported himself with free-lance writing and editing for the next ten years, and in 1987 he became involved in the democracy movement, eventually becoming secretary of the Executive Council of the NLD.

In June 1989, Win Tin was arrested by SLORC officials and charged with having a telephone conversation with the father of a girl who had had an illegal abortion. This bizarre charge suggests that Win Tin was actually arrested for his pro-democracy activities. During interrogation, he was repeatedly pressed to admit that he was Aung San Suu Kyi's "puppet master," but he refused to comment on these assertions and was sentenced to three years in prison. In 1992, weeks before the expiration of his sentence, Win Tin was sentenced to eleven more years in prison, reportedly because of his "links to foreign and insurgent organizations" and for "receiving money from foreign embassies."

In a letter published in a Japanese newspaper, Aung San Suu

Kyi describes her impressions of working with Win Tin:

> Win Tin is little given to talking about himself. As secretary and general secretary he and I worked closely on an almost daily basis from the time the NLD was founded, but it was several months before I discovered, quite by chance, that he was a bachelor who lived alone and managed his own household chores. Soon after he was sentenced in 1989, the lease on the state-owned flat where he had been living for many years was cancelled and friends had to move his possessions out of the apartment ... Win Tin's whole demeanor conveys such an impression of firmness, few people are aware that he suffers from a heart condition that requires constant medication. The long period spent in prison where medical care is inadequate and living conditions abysmal have aggravated his health problems ... In 1994, Win Tin wore a neck support: spondylitis has been added to his afflictions. He also is in need of dental support. But his mind [is] clear and his spirit upright and unwavering.

In November 1995, Win Tin circulated a petition among his fellow prisoners protesting the conditions within Rangoon's Insein Prison. Four months later, on March 28, 1996, he was sentenced to another five years' imprisonment for this act. His cumulative sentence is now due to expire in 2007—but who can say how many more years may be added in the next decade.

Because appeals to the SLORC have had no effect, and may even be counterproductive, human-rights groups have turned to multinational businesses with large-scale investments in Burma for help. Please write letters to Pepsi-Cola Corporation asking them to intervene on Win Tin's behalf at this address:

> Pepsi-Cola Corporation
> Consumer Affairs Department
> Routes 100 and 35
> Somers, NY 10589, USA

Thanks to Siobhan Dowd at PEN American Center in New York and Robin Jones at International PEN's Writers-in-Prison Committee in London for help researching this profile.

Judy Budnitz

I knew a wonderful secret back then.
I wish I could remember what it was.

Judy Budnitz graduated from Harvard in 1995 and then received a writing fellowship from the Fine Arts Work Center in Provincetown. Currently, she is taking part in NYU's graduate program in creative writing. Her stories have appeared in *The Paris Review* and *Story*.

Judy Budnitz

JUDY BUDNITZ

Hundred-Pound Baby

*T*here's a hundred-pound baby in the house that no one's talking about.

I can hear it thumping around. It's just a baby, too young to walk; it's crawling with its belly sliding across the linoleum. Sssssssssth. Sssssssssth.

I've tried to tell my mother. She says, Baby? The baby's right here. Kay, stop it. Don't eat that.

Kay is my sister. She won't eat anything you feed her on a spoon, but she'll eat anything she finds on the ground. She is red most of the time from screaming.

Not Kay, the other baby, I tell my mother. But she doesn't want to talk about it.

My mother got really big before Kay was born. Then she went to the hospital and we went to visit her, me and my dad. And we went to the room with the glass wall and the rows of babies and Kay was in there somewhere and my dad said isn't she a beauty and I said yeah, though I couldn't tell which was her.

Then my mother came home and she was still big. She stayed in bed with the pillows heaped around her and one under her knees. She had dark circles under her eyes like she'd been hit on the head.

She'd yell for me sometimes: Nick! Nicky! *Nicholas!* When I came in the shades would be down and the bed unmade and my mother puddled in the middle of it. Nick, would you turn on the TV, she'd say, I can't seem to rouse myself.

She was right. She was too heavy to get up. So I would turn on the little TV on her dresser and flip channels till she said stop, and I'd fiddle with the volume and the antenna until she was satisfied. Then she'd say, Bring me the *TV Guide*, will you? And I would bring it over to her. Up close her mouth had an unbrushed smell and her hair had a mousy smell, too.

If she saw dirt on my face she'd lick her finger and try to rub it off. I hated that. I'd try to get out of her room as fast as I could.

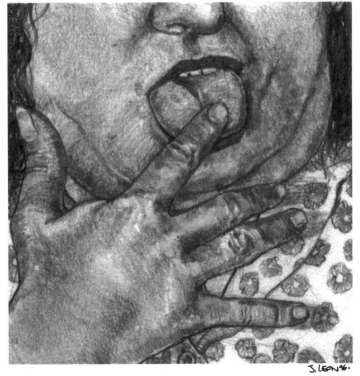

Could you come back in an hour and change it to channel seven? she'd yell after me.

Okay, okay, I'd say, and run down the stairs and go outside. I think the sky was always gray then, and heavy and low and not a breath of air stirring. The air was thick, humid; it made me want to pant like a dog. The sparkly summer insects, the moths and grasshoppers, were all gone by then. All that was left were those black gnats like bits of dirt that liked to fly in your eyes.

My dad bought me this kite with ninja warriors painted on it. It was supposed to do loops and tricks in the air but I could never get it off the ground. I had my friend Newt hold the string and I held the kite and we ran across the field behind the swimming pool. Again and again, back and forth. The air was too heavy and brooding to lift it. Once I lost my grip but Newt kept running and I ran after yelling, Stop, stop! I kept trying to grab it, but it was dragging along just beyond my fingers, catching and tearing on the dry grass.

Newt was not really my friend.

My mother kept Kay in a crib in the storage room off of their bedroom. One morning she yelled at me to come here. I came and found her shuffling around Kay's room in her slippers. Her nightgown was unbuttoned more than it should have been.

Kay was lying there wiggling around. So pink all over, and her arms and legs were so fat they had creases in them. Her eyes stayed closed most of the time and with her bald head and scrunched-up face she looked like a little old man.

I want to show you something, my mother said. She leaned into the crib and I saw her breasts swinging loose. She lifted Kay up, carried her to the changing table, and changed her diaper.

Now you do it, she told me. Take this one off and put on a new one.

Kay squalled. She didn't like going through it all again. Her body felt soft and trembly and loose. It felt like my face, my chin. She was so light. I could have picked her up by the ankles and swung her around and around over my head.

I tried to do it quick and it was like wrapping up raw meat, like chicken. It was not too hard because she was already clean. My mother looked satisfied as she went back to sink down in her hollow on the bed.

Afterwards my mother asked me to change Kay again and again. I started to wish I hadn't done such a good job that first time.

I stayed out of the house. It was so hot, but the sun wouldn't shine. It was so humid that it made sweat break out on your forehead and drip down your back. There was a creek near our house and I went there with Newt. It was down in a deep ravine and none of the kids in the neighborhood were supposed to go there. So we all did. Someone had tied a rope up in one of the trees and if you swung hard enough and jumped at the right moment you would land on the other side of the ravine. If you missed you'd go slipping and sliding on the loose dirt down the steep slopes and land in the creek. The creek was only a foot deep, but so murky it must have been full of tropical diseases.

My mother had said some kid broke his leg or back or head swinging on that thing, and I wasn't supposed to go there. I wondered why no one had cut down the rope then. I figured some of the parents went there secretly sometimes to swing on it. They liked to keep the secrets to themselves.

It was a wonderful swing, a wonderful flight-feeling to swing out and see the creek fifteen feet below, feel the dip and sway as the tree branch bent with the weight, the soft, floating moment after leaving the rope and before meeting the ground. Then the earth leapt upward with a knee-buckling crash landing on the other side.

Sometimes we went wading to catch crawdads or the little orange lizards that were named after Newt. People said there were leeches there. I didn't mind leeches, but I thought of the African worms I saw on TV that could bore into your foot and work their way into your stomach and get longer and longer inside you.

One day when I came home I found my mother sitting on the edge of the bed with her feet on the floor. Her hair was matted up. Her nightgown was unbuttoned again and slipping off one shoulder. I can't stand up and I can't lie down, she said. I can't seem to get my feet off the ground.

It almost sounded like a song I had heard somewhere.

Would you go check on Kay, honey? she said. She'd never called me honey before.

My dad was not around much.

My dad was an accountant and that meant lots of papers and wearing suits and migraine headaches. His hair was receding on the sides but not as fast in the middle. His hair was dark, and when he didn't shave for a day the stubble gave his face a gray shadow.

He and my mother used to touch each other a lot. Even at the dinner table. He liked to run his fingers through her hair and she would laugh and stroke his smooth forehead. Then they would lean over the table and kiss and afterwards I would have to check my plate for stray hairs.

He was happy that day in the hospital when he said, Isn't she a beauty? He said it the way he talked about cars or boats in magazines. Hushed. Isn't she something?

But soon after he changed. He stayed at his office later and when he came home he spent a long time drinking coffee and reading newspapers with very small print. My mother would not go out so he started buying the groceries: peanut butter and microwaveable TV dinners. He started sleeping downstairs on the living-room sofa. So Kay's crying wouldn't disturb him, he said. He was very busy, he needed his sleep, he told me.

I think it was my mother who disturbed him.

I know my dad bought me things like the kite to fill in the spaces. It didn't fly.

Then they started fighting. It started small and soft and then grew. My dad would sneak into the bedroom to get something from his closet and my mother would call from the bed, Steven, could you change the baby?

And he said, Why can't you?

I'm tired, she said, I was up all night with her.

And he said, I have to go to work, remember, and I'm trying to run this house and take care of the kid—and now you're asking me to change diapers? And what do you do besides lie around all day?

She said, Is it so hard to change your own daughter's diapers?

Why can't *you?* he growled back.

She curled herself in tighter and said, You, you don't understand.

You're right, he shouted, I don't understand how you can lay a guilt trip on me when you're the one who's such a goddamn lazy—

Don't talk like that in front of Nick, my mother said.

I didn't know the kid was here, my dad said. Nick, get out of here.

Wait, Nick. Could you go check on Kay? my mother said.

Kay was sort of whimpering and kicking her legs like she was swimming but she wasn't getting anywhere. She was very wet. She reminded me of my mother.

My father didn't like to see my mother lying in that dim room day after day in the same flowered nightgown with her face hanging slack. I didn't either. I went to the creek. Dad stayed later at the office, then he started going out for a drink with some of the other men.

Where have you been? my mother shrieked the first time.

Just stopped for a drink on the way home, he said. Very cold.

The next time she said, Where were you? And then, There's someone, isn't there?

Then my dad closed the door and I heard only the ups and downs of their voices. I got out of bed and went downstairs. It was dark and everything looked blue in the moonlight. I kept holding my breath, listening for something something something, and it seemed something was holding its breath, listening to me.

Soon after that my dad moved out. He said, Look, Nick, it's not permanent. Just until we sort some things out, okay? I'll still come visit, lots, and you can come see my apartment, and maybe I'll be back home when we work this out. Okay?

That's what Newt's dad told him last year. Now his mother works at the Quiki-Mart and she dates an old man with white hair and an accent and a glass eye. That's what happens.

Will you watch out for your sister? Your mom and your sister? my dad said.

Okay, okay, okay, I said.

After that my mother really got big. She'd never gone back to normal size after Kay and now she was growing like crazy. It was cooler outside and leaves were changing and shriveling and the sky was still gray, but now it was crisp and anxious. Inside, my mother swelled like bread rising. Twice a day and sometimes more she'd yell to me and when I came she'd give me some money from her purse and tell me to run to the store down the street. She asked for very particular things. Sometimes she was in a sweet mood, sometimes a salty one.

Now that my dad was gone she had groceries and Pampers delivered from the supermarket. I helped the delivery guy carry the bags in. Thanks, sport, he said. He had a big smile and a gold tooth. When we finished he hovered in the door for a while. Didn't you say your mother was home? he asked after a while, gazing up the stairs.

Yeah, but she won't come down, I told him.

His smile went away. It figures, he muttered as he let the screen door slam behind him.

My mother still sent me on daily trips because she wanted the plastic-wrapped, artificial sweet things you can only get at a place like the Quiki-Mart. Sometimes she asked for things neither I nor the man at the store had heard of. She must have eaten them when she was a kid. Gobstoppers, jujubes, Cracker Jack.

My mother told me I could get some junk if I wanted. But I couldn't stomach anything after seeing her plunge her fists into a bag, seeing her face all greasy with crumbs and powdered sugar and slow sweat.

What I liked to do was stick my finger in the peanut-butter jar and lick it off. And then do it again. I liked to think of everyone eating my germs and not knowing it. I stayed at the creek for hours looking at the water so dark and thick and decayed smelling.

School started up again, and third grade was worse than second grade was. We had to run laps during recess. They didn't let us put number lines on our desks to help with subtraction anymore. Someone kept stealing my lunch money out of my desk. I went straight to the creek after school.

My mother was huge and I noticed it all of a sudden one day. I had given her a bag with some pretzels and Twinkies and the change, and she looked at my face and said, Oh, honey, and hugged me. And my face pressed into her breast or her neck or her shoulder or her upper arm, I couldn't even tell, she was all one quivering, smothery mass. She gulped little sobs deep inside. I couldn't wait to get out.

She'd gotten big before Kay was born. And back then she'd been sort of tired and grouchy, and she'd cried sometimes. And she'd asked for strange things to eat.

Looked like she was going to have another baby. A big one.

My dad wasn't around so I thought I would have to act as a kind of father. I wasn't sure what I had to do. I wasn't sure I'd be able to pick the baby out from a roomful of babies the way my dad did.

I probably could. It would be the biggest baby in the room.

Aunt Sandra showed up then.

She was my mother's sister. She lived a ways away. We visited there last summer; it took us a day to drive. She had a big house and a husband who was a dentist and laughed a fake ho-ho-ho laugh. Aunt Sandra wore big rings and high heels and was fluttery like a bird. Her laugh was sharp and real, like a sneeze.

She came in without knocking, calling, Helloo, Helloo, anybody hooome? I came running down the stairs and she said, Nick! Nick! Where's your mother? Is she all right?

She's upstairs, I said. She's okay.

I haven't talked to her for weeks. I was so worried—I had to come out. Every time I called someone told me she couldn't come to the phone, Aunt Sandra said, glancing around.

Yeah, I said. She told me to say that to everyone that called. Even my dad.

Your dad ... ? she said and then clicked up the stairs in her high heels. I heard her go into the bedroom, heard her say, Helen? Helen? Oh, Hel—, and then the door closed and there was muffled talking and crying and the bed creaking beneath them.

Much much later Aunt Sandra came out and tapped at my door. Nick? she said. Nick, I think your mother needs a vacation. I'm going to take her away for a while.

Where? I said.

We'll go to my friend's lakehouse up in New Hampshire. It's beautiful, and she can relax there ... Nick, someone needs to stay here with you and your sister. Do you want me to ask your dad, or should I find a sitter?

A sitter, I said.

So that's what they did. Aunt Sandra had to buy my mother a new dress, her old ones didn't fit. My mother lumbered out of the house, not looking up, Aunt Sandra's arm around her shoulder. She was huge; Aunt Sandra was child-size next to her. They drove off under the gray sky and it was raining, so light you couldn't see it, but you could feel it tingling.

Mrs. Moore came to stay with us. Kay didn't like her. Neither did I. Kay didn't like her new formula, she kept spitting it up on

Mrs. Moore's shoulder. Mrs. Moore had stiff gray hair and big glasses and perfect posture. At night she snored. I walked around downstairs and nothing was there, but the snores and Kay's cries filled the darkness so it was not empty.

They were gone three weeks.

My mother came back changed. Her eyes were steadier. She laughed and her laugh was short and sharp. Her hair was smooth and shiny and when she hugged me I could tell her neck from her shoulder from her arm again. She was smaller and harder. Her stomach had gone down some.

She'd had the baby.

Look at your mother, doesn't she look great? said Aunt Sandra.

You've lost about a hundred pounds, I said.

My mother laughed at that. She had Kay in her arms. Kay looked like she might spit up any minute. Or maybe she was smiling.

They were all so happy looking I didn't want to ask about the new baby right then.

I know it's here. I can hear it. No one wants to talk about it. How can they ignore a hundred-pound baby?

My mother drinks diet milkshakes. When I ask her if I can have one she says, No. We grown-ups get all the good stuff. Those are the rules.

When we are downstairs the baby is upstairs. When we are in Kay's room I hear it crawling on the kitchen floor. Sssssssssth. Sssssssssth.

Baby? Here's the baby, right here, my mother says, thrusting Kay at me. Kay smiles for real. She has a head full of hair and spit bubbles on her smile.

Not Kay, I say. The other one. The big one you had.

Don't tell me you want another baby. One in the house is enough, my mother says.

My mother takes classes at night now, and Mrs. Moore returns to sit. She sits straight upright, as if something has startled her.

My father used to stop by once a week. Now he doesn't come at all.

My mother is busy all the time: she rushes around, she changes all the diapers. She stays out of bed. Her feet are never still. She is too happy. Her smile is strained. There is tension heavy in the house, phone conversations buzzing behind closed doors—something is waiting to happen.

It's that baby. Babies don't like to be ignored. He must be wet by now; someone should change him; I'd do it if he would stay still and let me find him.

My mother smiles hard at me but does not tell me anything. She calls me honey now and then. She knows about the baby and she won't tell me. She must be the one feeding it and changing it, changing the big hundred-pound diapers. She talks on the phone to Aunt Sandra lots, but she won't talk to me. All secretive. The parents keep all the good things for themselves. Isn't a hundred-pound baby a good thing? All babies are good things, so a really big one must be even better.

He's like a turtle with the big head waving around and the big stomach holding him down and baby hands swimming in the air. I worry about him being hungry so I pour some of Kay's formula into three bowls and leave them in different places around the house.

The next day my mother says, What's that smell? Nick? Did you do this?

I hear my mother talking on the phone: … I don't want him in this house anymore … get rid of him as soon as possible … I don't want him seeing Nick, either …

So she is hiding the baby from me. But she doesn't want him herself. No wonder he stays so quiet, never cries. He knows he'll get thrown out.

My mother takes long, hot showers. She buys new clothes and high heels like Aunt Sandra. I see her dusting with a rag torn from the flowered nightgown. She is always busy, in and out, on the phone. The hundred-pound baby dodges her. So do I.

I hear her on the phone again, saying: I need to tell him ... he needs to know ...

She's going to break the news to the baby. He can't hide forever.

One afternoon in November my mother comes to me all serious and stern. Nick, she says, your father and I are getting a divorce. Do you know what that means?

I say yeah.

We both love you, Nick. And we still like each other. We're still friends. But we need to spend less time together. Do you understand that? It's ... it's like your friend Newt. He's your friend, isn't he, but I haven't seen him come over here for a long time. But he's still your friend, isn't he? Sometimes friends need to be apart. Don't they?

I think of Newt dragging the new kite through the weeds and brush. I remember it sliding along jaggedly right in front of me, just out of reach. It is shredded and broken, it will never fly.

Nick, I want you to think about something. Do you want to live here with me and your sister, or would you like to live with your dad? I want you here and Kay wants you here. Do you want to stay?

My mother has two lines between her eyebrows.

I don't want to talk about that; I try to turn away but she grabs my arm.

Okay, okay, I say, twisting away from her. It is not hard to say; I decided that a long time ago. Okay.

The hundred-pound baby comes to me that night. I can't see him, it's too dark, but I can hear his breathing like soft hiccups. He whimpers beside the bed, he thumps against it, shaking me.

He's saying, Me, me, me, what about me? Can I stay? What about me?

He doesn't say it but that's what he means, I can tell. I have learned from reading Kay.

I reach down to touch him, give him a pat maybe, but he is already lumping away. I can see his shadow cross the hall. He's crying, crying, crying; his tears leave a wet path behind him like a snail's trail.

After things get all settled and arranged, my dad comes back to get the rest of his things: the tennis racquets in the basement, the encyclopedias he won as a prize in high school. He's growing a beard now, a grayish-brown scruff all over his face. All you can see are his eyes.

I help him put books in boxes and carry them to his car. I remember the delivery guy with the gold tooth who called me sport. I remember his face.

I'll miss you, Nick, my dad said in between trips.

You can still visit if you want, I said and shrugged. It's okay with me.

I'm moving to Chicago, Nick, my dad said. But I can still call. I'll want to talk to you. You can come visit on vacations. It'll be fun.

Well, it's good I decided not to live with you, I say, because I wouldn't want to switch schools and all that.

You decided? But I never asked for custod—, he said and caught himself. I mean … Nick, I meant that I …Christ, Nick, that's not what I meant …

That is all. While he's inside saying good-bye to my mother I slip one of Kay's dirty diapers into an open box in his trunk. Then he comes out and puts his hand on the back of my neck and gives it a squeeze and a shake. That's good-bye.

He drives off with his car coughing and growling. I go down to the ravine.

The rope swing is still there. The sun comes through the trees in sudden jabs and splotches. Down below, way down there, a million miles down, is the creek. Trickle-drip-drip, wet rocks and tropical diseases. That's where it all goes. Down. Can't get my feet off the ground. Can't change the channel. Can't get up. My mother was right.

I yank on the rope. The branch bends. It creaks like bed-springs. Nothing holds up. You can't fight gravity. You can't ever fly.

I jump up anyway.

I jump and the swing holds, it holds together, I swing back and forth, higher and higher and my feet aren't touching the ground higher and higher until I can make it across the gap the creek will not get me and now is the time to let go for the floating swimming feeling before the slamming crash landing.

Kay would like it. I will show her one day.

When I go home it feels like a hundred-pound weight has lifted. That baby is gone.

Where's the baby? I ask my mother.

Right here, says my mother. Look, Kay, there's Nicky. Kay looks up at me and gives me a smile. A big gummy one. She is getting better and better at smiling. So is my mother. I think the baby must have slipped into my dad's car when no one was looking. Won't he be surprised, halfway to Chicago, to find a hundred-pound baby in the backseat.

Short-Story Award for New Writers
1st-, 2nd-, and 3rd-Place Winners

•❖ *1st place* and $1200 to *Ami Silber*, for "Pacific"
Silber's profile appears on page 130 and her story begins on page 131.

•❖ *2nd place* and $500 to *Erwin Rosinberg*, for "Medical History"
Erwin Rosinberg is a first-year undergraduate student at Harvard University and is pursuing a degree in English. He would like to thank his family, friends, and teachers. If successful as a writer, he does not plan to be a recluse in New Hampshire.

Erwin Rosinberg

Erwin Rosinberg
"Medical History"

Ellen's groom, the doctor, said he'd recommend a podiatrist as soon as they returned from the honeymoon, but that he himself wouldn't treat any family members. Hilda whispered to a fat woman in a yellow dress that having a doctor in the family was the whole point of the wedding, and that she wouldn't have given Ellen her blessing if she knew the husband was going to be dead weight.

•❖ *3rd place* and $300 to *Rose Allison*, for "Redemption"
Rose Allison is a free-lance copywriter and graphic artist in Oklahoma City, OK. After more than fifteen years of writing to please clients, she started writing to please herself. She didn't know how hard that would be.

Rose Allison

Rose Allison
"Redemption"

*Paul cut off his hand in April as a morning sun shone golden on the pale new leaves of blooming crab-apple and redbud trees. He placed his left wrist in the padded curve he had spent four weeks creating and released the blade that hung above it.
The blade was sharp; it was a clean cut.*

We thank all entrants for sending in their work.

Ami Silber

*My subtle system of passive aggression being developed in
the backyard of our Southern California home.*

Ami Silber is a first-year Ph.D. candidate at the University of California, San Diego in the Literature Department, where she studies seventeenth- and eighteenth-century British literature. Several of her short plays have appeared on college stages, including the Chautauqua Festival at UC Santa Cruz. She wrote featured columns for *City on a Hill Press* and the *Santa Cruz Sentinel*. This is her first published work of short fiction.

AMI SILBER
Pacific

FIRST-PLACE WINNER
Short-Story Award
for New Writers

*E*ven though I am three months shy of my fifteenth
birthday, I can drive a car as well as or better than most people
twice my age. I can also drive at night without headlights. I don't
even bump over the raised markers in the road, either. Lots of
practice has given me some kind of strange instinct—it's like I
can *feel* where the road is going to turn next, or how deep and
how long the curve will be. Another thing is that I can read in
a moving car. Not just browse through a magazine, but really
read a book and remember important details. It doesn't matter
if we're driving through rain, or up a winding mountain. I don't
get sick, also, on long car trips.

These are all skills I've gotten over the past year and a half, ever
since my mom and I left Columbus. Once my stepdad had
packed up his things and cleared out, Mom took a good long
look around our house and decided she wanted to leave. For
good this time. She took the two vinyl suitcases out of the garage,
the orangey-plaid ones with the broken locks. Mom got one
suitcase and I got the other. What we couldn't fit in the suitcases
got left behind, including the record player and television and
the cat, which didn't come home much anyway.

She locked the door of the house while I waited in the
passenger seat of our Dodge Dart.

"Okay, Isadora, get your seat belt fastened," she said, adjusting the driver's seat. My stepdad was the one who drove the car the most. He never let my mom take the car on her own, and dropped her off wherever she wanted to go. The beauty parlor, the movies, the grocery store. Then she would have to call him at home to get picked up. Sometimes he wouldn't come to get her for almost two hours. Which is why we never had ice cream at home.

"We're not stopping until we're out of Columbus," Mom warned me.

"I know," I said. "I went to the bathroom already. Did you turn off the television?"

"Yes ... No ... Doesn't make much difference, anyway. We won't be around to pay the electric bill."

"I guess not."

That's what we said to each other when we pulled out of the driveway and away from the house we'd lived in for just about all my life. The funny thing is that thinking back on it now, I can't remember very much about that house. Not the way the rooms met or where they faced, and not the color of the couch. All I remember is the peeling, flowered shelf paper that lined my dresser. The smell of it was plastic and flat.

What I know now is this car. I know its shape on the outside and the textures on the inside. The cracked dashboard and the pilled floormats and the grooves the plastic seats leave on the backs of my legs. And I know the frustrated engine as it pulls itself up a hill, and the gasp of the air conditioner which we use even though it only blows hot air. Sometimes Mom and I stay in motels, but usually we sleep in the car. It's been our home for the past year and a half as we take the long way across the country. That's what Mom calls it. The long way.

Once, we had maps, but they got so crumpled and faded that we threw them away in a Dumpster in Memphis. Then Mom took me to eat barbecue and listen to jazz music at a small, muggy restaurant to celebrate. She took me by my hands and we danced around the table while everybody clapped. Then we got a free order of ribs which we ate out of their paper bag in the backseat of the car at midnight. There was barbecue sauce everywhere, but we didn't even have the old maps to wipe our faces off. My sides hurt from laughing so hard. They still ached the next morning.

Once, maybe, the car was clean and orderly. Now it's filled with the bits that make up our life here. Our clothes still fit in the two suitcases, but there are also magazines, tubes of sunscreen, three ceramic cups, a salt shaker, pencil shavings, overdue library books from just about every state. And in my jeans pocket—the jeans I wash myself—is a souvenir key ring from San Diego. It used to belong to my dad, my real dad. Though my mom talks not at all about him, I know that he was in the military and he was stationed in San Diego, and the thing he loved more than anything was the ocean. Aside from movies and TV, I've never actually seen the ocean. The key ring has a little beach scene painted on it, and I've stared at it for hours, looking at the waves forever cresting and falling onto the sand. I think about the warm, salty water and wonder what it would feel like on my skin. It must be different from being in a pool, because in a pool you know there is a beginning and an end. But the ocean stretches and stretches, and I might be standing on the beach in San Diego and the edge of the ocean could reach all the way to Sydney or Singapore, but that still would not take into account all the other places it goes.

This is an idea I've taken and petted and worried over. The big, wide ocean that doesn't care about you or where you've been. All it cares about is what it knows—and it's older than everything, so it knows a lot. Maybe this idea might be scary or too large for some people, but for me, I have the big ocean in the back of my mind. It sits there and is always watching, always keeping its tides and ebbs, and to me, that is comforting, like when my mom sings to me late at night the songs she knew when she was a little girl. My favorite is "Can't Help Falling in Love with You."

The reason why I know how to drive is simple. There are lots of times when Mom just can't drive. She doesn't feel good mostly, or she's cranky or tired, and sometimes I've gotten her out of a bar where she goes to find company. Then she leans against me, and I'm always surprised how heavy she is because to me she is my skinny mom in cutoffs, and not an oversized barfly. I put her in the passenger seat with the window rolled down and soft country music on the radio, which she likes when she doesn't feel so good. Then I drive away with the headlights off to avoid being followed. That's how I learned to do that. Lots of times guys follow Mom out of the bar and they think that a fourteen-year-old girl isn't too much trouble, that I won't keep them from getting what they want, so they try to catch up with us.

Before I learned the trick of driving without lights, a few guys did catch up with us. I'll just say that it's a good thing my mom can barf at will, because otherwise there might have been trouble. The problem with this solution was that it sure did smell bad, and cleaning Mom up is pretty hard, especially if she starts talking about what she calls her lost direction and all that sort of stuff. After a few drinks, she gets on that subject and I can only listen, because what can I say? So I can drive at night without headlights and even without lights on the street, too, that's how good at it I am.

Lately, Mom has gone on more benders than usual. I think it's because we are going to visit her parents, which brings back things she doesn't want to think about. I don't know much about them, my grandparents, since I have never seen a picture of them, and they never called or visited when we lived in Columbus. Since we've been on our way to see them, I have been thinking a lot about them, and about why my mom is so

134   *Glimmer Train Stories*

afraid of them, and if they are friendly or mean or even if I look like them at all. I have one photo of my real dad which was taken just before he was killed in a training exercise, but it's blurry and he's squinting into the bright sun, so it's hard to make out his face. He's smiling, though.

The thing is, why go to see my grandparents if it causes everyone so much trouble? My mom in particular, I mean. She likes to talk about everything she sees, smoking cigarettes and drinking bottled water, but she won't talk about where she's been. About my dad and how they met, or about what her parents wanted her to do after high school. Maybe this is why I can't recall much about life in Columbus, because she has drawn a cloth over it that I am not allowed to pull back.

We are finally in California, which is where my grandparents live. I drove across the Nevada border last night as Mom slept in the backseat, and when she woke up, we were crossing the hot open fields of central California. I heard Mom groan and try to pull our little blanket over her head. The light here is strong, stronger than any other place we've been. It fills my eye sockets and makes them sticky, so you can imagine that when Mom woke up and found herself flooded with this gluey light, and her head not feeling too good to begin with, she wasn't very happy.

"Here's the Pepto," I said, pulling our bottle out of the glove compartment. Without turning around, I pressed the bottle into her waiting hand. I felt, for a second, the beginning of softness in her hand, the kind of loose softness in an old woman's hand.

"This is it, this is my last hangover," she said, and took a swig from the bottle. "Don't give me that look, Isadora, because I am deadly earnest this time. But what a night! You ought to have been there. It was something out of a cheap drive-in movie. Do you recall that fellow Earl, the one who changed the oil at the filling station? He was there and taunting me with this … I don't know … *proprietary* air, if you get me. Which didn't sit well with some of the other fellows, and then their lady friends didn't seem pleased about that fact, either. And I just went to the ladies' room for a minute. A minute, I mean it, just to touch up my lipstick, and when I got back, the place had just exploded! Chairs and bottles and even—get this—a cowboy boot, a *ladies'* cowboy boot. All over the bar. Oh, it was a perfect riot, perfect." She laughed until her headache made her stop, and she pressed the cool plastic bottle to her temple.

I'll admit it, it made me sad to think of Mom losing her elastic self with her softening hands in the middle of a bar fight. She's not the kind of mom who'd make her daughter say she was the older sister. She doesn't pretend, if you know what I mean, that she is anybody except who she is. When her fellows are around, she likes to have me with her, and she says, "This is my daughter," with her chin up like she's challenging them to take issue. And if someone does, she tells them to take a hike.

That happened once in Oklahoma. I went into the bar because my mom says to get her after three hours. Three hours, she says, is enough to get whatever needs to be accomplished taken care of. After that, it's just excessive. So I went into the bar after the three hours like she said, and by this point, it was close to closing time so there weren't a lot of people around. The bar looked like a lot of bars, nothing set it apart, except there was a collection of teeth kept in a big jar behind the bartender. Mom was leaned over the sticky black bar with a drink cupped in her hands, and she was laughing with some cowboy. That didn't mean much to me, because Mom has said to me that laughing sets someone off-guard, in case you want to lose them or get a punch in. So I thought I'd see if she wanted to go for real.

The two of them went on for a while, him barking out some joke and her going along with it, and I stood at the guy's elbow waiting for Mom to notice me.

"Hey, kid, this ain't the right place for you," the cowboy said to me once he saw me. He didn't say it in a mean way, but I could tell he wanted to get down to business and couldn't with me standing there.

"Wait a minute, Kyle," my mom cut in, "that's my daughter. That's Isadora."

"Your daughter?" He looked at me again, closer this time, and the laugh lines in the corners of his eyes tightened because he wasn't laughing so much anymore. "You're kidding, right? Helen, you're kidding."

"I surely am not." She took a sip of her drink. "Isadora, say hello to Kyle."

I nodded.

"She don't say much."

"No, Isadora's what you'd call a thinker. A deep thinker. She's my conscience." Mom thought this idea was funny, and she giggled into her melting ice. "She's my Jiminy Cricket."

While Mom was swirling her drink around, Kyle leaned over to me. I saw the dark flecks where his whiskers were coming in after his evening shave, and the beer smell was on him and in his clothes. "Listen, Isadora, or Jiminy, or whatever you're called," he said to me, "you're not going to keep on standing here, are you? You're not going to hang around? I don't like kids much."

"I'm just waiting for my mom," I said. "And I'm not a kid, so it doesn't matter to me if you like kids or not."

He turned back to Mom. "You want another one, honey?" he asked her.

She threw back the rest of her drink, which was mostly water at that point. "I've had my limit for tonight."

"Maybe we can go someplace else, then."

"No thanks."

She moved past him, but he took hold of her arm. "Are you sure about that?" he said, and Mom looked up at him right in his eyes.

"I am quite sure, thanks for your consideration."

He nodded his head in my direction. "It's not 'cause of her? I mean, we could tell her to get lost for a while, if that's the problem."

"I think it's time you let go of me."

He did, and he left without saying anything else. Once he had gone, Mom slumped down on a barstool. She blew her breath out through her hair and ran her thumbs along the zipper of her purse.

"Do you think you could get the car started, Isadora? I just want to splash some water on my face and then I'll come out."

"Sure."

I went out and heard the cicadas in the brush, and the gravel of the parking lot under my feet. When I got to the car, I took out the keys, but then I was pushed up against the door, and the cool metal roof pressed against my cheek as I tried to breathe. The weight of a man's body pinned me, and his fingers dug into my hair and into my ear.

"I don't much care for kids, I said, and I particularly don't care for kids who get in my way," he said. He pulled my head back, and I couldn't see him, just the neon sign of the bar. I was just about as tall as he was, but I knew that even if I tried, there wasn't much I could do to get him off me.

I waited for him to turn me around or hit me, like my step-dad had sometimes done, but that didn't happen. Mom had somehow found a two-by-four, and she came out of the bar and cracked it against his head. I heard her screaming and cursing, and he let go of me to hold his arms up to cover himself. She hit him and hit him as he crouched down, and when she looked satisfied, she got into the passenger seat and I started the car and we drove away. In the rearview mirror, I saw him stagger to his feet and back into the bar.

"Pull over," she said after a few minutes, and I did so.

She lit a cigarette, and I could see from the lighter that her face was wet and her hands shook. Rolling down the window, she tossed the cigarette out.

"You're okay, aren't you, Isadora?"

"Yeah, he didn't do anything."

"Come here a minute, would you?"

Without waiting for me to come over, she reached out and wrapped her arms around me tight. Her bones were so easy to feel through her tank top, and her shaking felt like the shaking of a thin white birch.

"Oh my baby," she said into my hair. "My baby, baby girl. This is no life for you. What the hell am I thinking? What are we doing here, anyway?"

"Don't worry about me," I said. "I'm fine, and we're fine."

"This can't be enough for you."

"It's plenty. I'm glad for it."

She kissed the top of my head and let me go, rubbing her face with her hands. "You're sure you're okay?"

"Mom, you really whupped that guy."

Then she laughed, a real laugh. "I did, didn't I?" she asked proudly. "Not too shabby for an old lady, huh?"

"Better than Pro Wrestling," I said, and we both laughed.

So maybe you think she is no good, but she is who I know, and she is the only other inhabitant of my small world—the world that is this car and the road we are traveling on.

Do you know that book *The Little Prince*? Do you remember how the Prince lives on a tiny, tiny planet that could fit inside a swimming pool? And there is only the Prince and his Rose on this planet, and all he does all day is take care of the Rose and make sure the baobab trees don't take over. And so there's the Prince whose big job is watching out after the collapsible planet and tending a helpless, demanding Rose. When the Rose begins to turn brown, then what? When the Prince can't help the Rose anymore, then what happens to him? The Prince can't just get another Rose. It doesn't work that way. So where does he go?

Since that night in Oklahoma, though, we have driven with a kind of purpose, and instead of taking just any connection on the highway, Mom has given me directions, or she just drives the car herself. She has never spoken to me about just why we left

Columbus, or how long we would drive for, but it seemed to me after Oklahoma that everything that came before was like preparation for something. Maybe Mom thought it would be like a fresh start, because for a while, she avoided bars. But then we got closer to California, and I could feel the fear coming out of her, and soon I was back to the three-hour rule.

We have pulled into a giant parking lot in an outdoor mini-mall. Mom comes over with a shopping bag from the grocery store and hands me a box of doughnuts.

"Is this breakfast?" I ask, opening the box.

"For now," she says. "I just had chocolate-covered doughnuts when I woke up."

"You'd better eat them fast," I say, "or they're going to melt in the heat."

"That's the best part. Licking off the chocolate icing and tossing the doughnut away." She shows me.

"Why not just get a chocolate bar, then?"

"Don't start with me, Isadora. Just don't even start." Annoyed, she grabs the box of doughnuts from my hands and throws them onto the ground, so the doughnuts fall out and roll under the other parked cars.

I go back to the grocery store and buy a box of cereal and a small carton of milk. For myself, I get an apple, because I don't much like breakfast food. While Mom sits on the bumper of the car and digs into the cereal box, she looks around at the mini-mall, squinting in the heat and confusion.

"So where are we, anyway?" she asks.

"I don't know, I think Salinas or something."

"So we'll be there today, huh?"

"I guess ... You've been there before, so you'd know better than me."

Her cheeks are full of cereal, but she still manages to frown. "Yeah, we'll be there real soon. A couple of hours."

"They know we're coming, right?"

"They know."

"Are you done with the cereal?"

"Is that a beauty parlor over there?"

"I think so."

"Let's go."

"What about—?"

"They can wait an hour or two longer. Suddenly, I'm just dying for a permanent."

"But your hair looks fine." It's long and light brown, like mine, though some have called my hair stringy.

She is already halfway across the parking lot, though, so she doesn't hear me.

While Mom gets her hair permed, I walk around the shopping mall. Outside the drugstore, there is a kid riding in a little coin-operated helicopter ride that grinds up and down. I watch him for a while, then go inside to look at the magazines. All the drugstores seem the same to me, even the employees in their red vests and bored faces are the same, but this doesn't give me the same kind of comfort that the constant ocean gives me. I almost forgot that I would see the ocean for the first time today, and even though I'm flipping through the teenage magazines, I can't ditch the anxiety curling inside my stomach. It's as if I'm afraid the ocean will push me away somehow, that it won't want me. What if it turns flat and glassy and hard when I try to touch it? What if everything that lives within it rots before I get there?

The time is up to get Mom from the beauty parlor. And the security guy has been trailing me around the drugstore since I've been here for about two hours without buying a single thing. I step into the chemical-smelling beauty parlor, and I see a blond woman standing in front of me turning back and forth. Her hair lies in tight curls to her shoulders, and she's talking to me. It takes me a minute to realize that this stranger with the blond hair is my mom. She's smiling at me and the beautician.

"What do you think, Isadora? Like a movie star, huh? I look just like someone in the movies. This is someone I ought to be."

The beautician chews her gum and nods.

I feel tricked. I hate Mom so much at this moment, my eyes sting. I've never hated her so much as I do now. Even if some words could come out of my tight throat, I wouldn't be able to speak to her.

"What's the matter, honey?" Mom asks me. The look of concern on her face makes me feel sick inside. "Don't you like it?"

I think about the Pacific Ocean waiting for me. "Can we go now?" I ask. Even to me, my voice sounds terrible and growled.

We don't speak in the car. I've turned myself away from her and stare out the passenger window. She's uncomfortable, and I'm glad for it. I want her to feel bad, as though her unhappiness gives me the same kind of pleasure as poking a bruise. I'm even more angry because she's spoiled my first look at the ocean. Since it's later in the day, the sun makes it look white, so I can barely look at it. All I can see is this giant white banner stretched from one side to the other. I can't feel anything for it, though, and I feel as white and sharp as the ocean. It's my hatred of Mom right now that makes me feel this way, I'm sure.

"It's beautiful, Isadora, isn't it?"

I don't want Mom to think I've forgiven her, so I just make a noise that's not a yes or a no.

"I grew up looking at this ocean, you know. Grandma and Grandpa's house sits right on the edge of a hill where you can always see it, and you learn its colors and its moods. My favorite is when it turns hard grey in the winter, and then the sun comes out a little and shines upon it like something out of a biblical epic. Like God's saying, 'Hey, get this.'" She glances over at me, but I'm careful to keep myself blank, so she continues. "You know what? You know why this ocean has its name? It's because when the Spanish came here four hundred years ago, they saw it, and it looked so welcoming. Because, you know, they'd come a long way across the deserts, and they were sick and thirsty and scared. Imagine being so far away from home. So think, all this desert, and then, boom! here's this great big ocean. They called it *Pacifica*—peaceful, calm. That's something, isn't it? The Pacific Ocean. It's such a relief to see after a long distance. Don't you feel it?"

It's suddenly so obvious to me why we're here, why Mom and I are on this road with the tall mustard plants growing beside it and the curves of the coastline and the solitary farms. I know why we've driven so far, and why Mom has changed her hair so she looks like somebody else, and why I'll never be able to say the right thing to her. I know this as well as I know how to drive this car, which I will soon leave forever.

I think back on the phone calls Mom made from pay phones while I waited in the car. She was talking to her parents, my grandparents, and making arrangements for my coming. If I turned to her now, if I said that she was wrong and if only she'd keep me with her she would find her sense of direction, would it make a difference? Could I stop her if I said something? And if I didn't, how could I bear it when there was the sudden emptiness I knew would follow?

To look at the ocean, I have to look at Mom. My eyes want to bounce off her because she is and is not my mom, with her new hair and her same face. That's what she wants. But I look at just her face to keep her the same to me, and see her eyes focusing on the road. My mind takes a little photo of her against the backdrop of the ocean and I think of them as my two forces. The way gravity is a force, so is my mom and so is the ocean to me in their constant presence and separation. But the water, which is what it is after all, just water and minerals mixed together, is fixed and will never turn away from me. After I am left with my grandparents, I know that I won't see Mom again, not for many years. By the time she comes back, I will have grown up, and not the span of the ocean nor the space in the front seat of a car could ever measure the distance between us.

The
Last
Pages

Blanche Howland with her son, George, beside a lake in New York State, 1946.

*A*nd these are two "after" pictures, my brother Carl at age three just before he died, his sweet courage as he sticks his finger in his ear, his fierce tenacity as he takes aim with his red dart gun at someone, probably my brother John, or me.

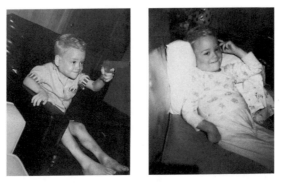

I've tried for years to write about my brother's illness, the most difficult writing assignment I've ever given myself, a mine field of potential sentimentality and unresolved grief.

Right after I wrote this story, I told a massage therapist about it while she worked the chronically sore muscles in my lower back.

"I lost my little brother, too," she said, "in much the same way." Then she told me about her brother's illness and death, pressing her thumbs hard into the hard knot of muscles that fisted at the base of my spine. "I don't know what is down here," she said, "but it's deep and it's been here a long time. Time to let it go, don't you think?" And then as if she'd flipped a switch, I began to weep. I completely lost it. I went on and on, tried again and again to stop, but couldn't.

If he'd lived, my brother would have turned thirty-five this July. I can only think of him as eternally three.

MARY OVERTON

*M*y dad and mom are happily retired in Florida now, in a lovely, modern, airy home far from rural Missouri. The photograph is of my grandfather, Pearl Overton, with his workhorses Joe and Queen. It was taken sometime in 1940. During the 1930s, Pearl often worked on other farms for a dollar a day. My dad remembers keeping butter and milk cool by putting them down the well. He speculates that he held his first book when he went to first grade.

JUDY BUDNITZ

*W*here do babies come from? It's a question I've read about and written about for a long time, and I've never come up with a really satisfactory explanation. That is, I hadn't until I moved to New York. The other day I woke up early and looked out the window, and discovered my neighbor's secret:

KEVIN CANTY

I think of my childhood as a Golden Age, perfect and frozen and out of time. Not perfect as in rosy—there were tears, drama, I broke my brother's thumb once—but perfect as in complete, finished. A childhood picture seems to come not so much from another time as from another *kind* of time, before the world started, like the Elgin marbles or a flint arrowhead.

Now I have children of my own, though, living through their own Golden Age. I look at my son Turner sometimes—he's seven—and I think, *That was when I fell off the horse. I spent two weeks in Inverness that summer.* But there's nothing perfect (finished, complete) about my son's world. I mean, he's chipper, he's smart, and he's relatively happy, but if you look at his drawing, the only living thing is all teeth and claws. My son is a small person in a large, confusing world.

The difficulty of childhood: A couple of weeks after writing "Flipper" I read it out loud to a couple of hundred people. I was astonished when they laughed. I was outraged. Later on, though, I thought, *What else are you going to do with it?*

150

MARY GORDON

*T*he poor you always have with you," Jesus said, but he was using these words as an excuse not to attend to them. Suppose you are afraid of not being one of the poor? Suppose you feel that this puts you in danger?

It is impossible to live in New York and to forget about the poor. It is impossible for a woman to feel that she is guaranteed a life of prosperity. It is impossible, therefore, not to feel afraid of prosperity.

This story is about women, friendship, New York, politics, aging, sex, terror, and pleasure. Its openness of form, I'd hoped, might begin to contain these disparate and yet united subjects.

Mary

ALICE MATTISON

Four years ago I wrote a story about Ida's roommate, then two about Ida, but I didn't understand what was happening until, in a story about entirely different people, a man I thought I didn't know picked up his daughter at work and when he walked in I recognized him: an old lover of Ida's.

I kept writing them, and something unexplained in each story led me to the next. Ida's in six of them, Tom's in four, other people come and go. When I reached this one, the last, I was nervous about whether the characters would come through for me. I hoped Ida and Tom would get together and I hoped various other people would show up. In another story, somebody gives a panhandler a twenty-dollar bill, and I had a feeling that my characters knew why; I hoped they'd let me in on that secret.

The baby in the story is named Jane after my dear friend Jane Kenyon, who died in 1995.

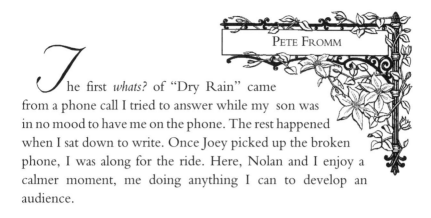

PETE FROMM

The first *whats?* of "Dry Rain" came from a phone call I tried to answer while my son was in no mood to have me on the phone. The rest happened when I sat down to write. Once Joey picked up the broken phone, I was along for the ride. Here, Nolan and I enjoy a calmer moment, me doing anything I can to develop an audience.

AMI SILBER

"Pacific" has several origins—mental snapshots, I guess—which contributed to its coming to be. I spent much of last year driving up and down the California coast between San Francisco and Santa Cruz, which lent itself to a good background for a story. Having just graduated from college and entering into "the real world" in the big city, I kept running back to old comforts. And then I also remember a conversation I had with my father in a taxicab in Mexico City not that long ago, which provided some of the underpinnings to this story.

Both of these origins were strongly visual—the coast with its recollections of Steinbeck film adaptations or Thomas Hart Benton paintings, and a Central American city literally on the verge of collapse. Having visual cues is important to me when I write; I need something to return to.

I knew I wanted to include a little sketch of Isadora, our teenage narrator, so I threw this drawing together specifically for this publication. She looks a little older than fourteen, but I guess that's to be expected.

And finally, this story is dedicated to my own mother and the road trips we've taken together.

PAST CONTRIBUTING AUTHORS AND ARTISTS
Issues 1 through 21 are available for eleven dollars each.

Robert H. Abel • Steve Adams • Susan Alenick • Rosemary Altea • A. Manette Ansay • Margaret Atwood • Aida Baker • Brad Barkley • Kyle Ann Bates • Richard Bausch • Robert Bausch • Charles Baxter • Ann Beattie • Barbara Bechtold • Cathie Beck • Kristen Birchett • Melanie Bishop • Corinne Demas Bliss • Valerie Block • Harold Brodkey • Danit Brown • Kurt McGinnis Brown • Paul Brownfield • Evan Burton • Gerard Byrne • Jack Cady • Annie Callan • Kevin Canty • Peter Carey • Carolyn Chute • George Clark • Dennis Clemmens • Evan S. Connell • Tiziana di Marina • Junot Díaz • Stephen Dixon • Michael Dorris • Siobhan Dowd • Barbara Eiswerth • Mary Ellis • James English • Tony Eprile • Louise Erdrich • Zoë Evamy • Nomi Eve • Edward Falco • Michael Frank • Pete Fromm • Daniel Gabriel • Ernest Gaines • Tess Gallagher • Louis Gallo • Kent Gardien • Ellen Gilchrist • Peter Gordon • Elizabeth Graver • Paul Griner • Elizabeth Logan Harris • Marina Harris • Erin Hart • Daniel Hayes • David Haynes • Ursula Hegi • Andee Hochman • Alice Hoffman • Jack Holland • Noy Holland • Lucy Honig • Linda Hornbuckle • David Huddle • Stewart David Ikeda • Lawson Fusao Inada • Elizabeth Inness-Brown • Andrea Jeyaveeran • Charles Johnson • Wayne Johnson • Thom Jones • Cyril Jones-Kellet • Elizabeth Judd • Jiri Kajanë • Hester Kaplan • Wayne Karlin • Thomas E. Kennedy • Jamaica Kincaid • Lily King • Maina wa Kinyatti • Marilyn Krysl • Frances Kuffel • Anatoly Kurchatkin • Victoria Lancelotta • Doug Lawson • Jon Leon • Doris Lessing • Janice Levy • Christine Liotta • Rosina Lippi-Green • David Long • Salvatore Diego Lopez • William Luvaas • Jeff MacNelly • R. Kevin Maler • Lee Martin • Eileen McGuire • Gregory McNamee • Frank Michel • Alyce Miller • Katherine Min • Mary McGarry Morris • Bernard Mulligan • Abdelrahman Munif • Sigrid Nunez • Joyce Carol Oates • Tim O'Brien • Vana O'Brien • Mary O'Dell • Elizabeth Oness • Peter Parsons • Annie Proulx • Jonathan Raban • George Rabasa • Paul Rawlins • Nancy Reisman • Linda Reynolds • Anne Rice • Roxana Robinson • Stan Rogal • Frank Ronan • Elizabeth Rosen • Janice Rosenberg • Kiran Kaur Saini • Libby Schmais • Natalie Schoen • Jim Schumock • Barbara Scot • Amy Selwyn • Bob Shacochis • Evelyn Sharenov • Floyd Skloot • Lara Stapleton • Barbara Stevens • William Styron • Liz Szabla • Paul Theroux • Patrick Tierney • Abigail Thomas • Randolph Thomas • Joyce Thompson • Andrew Toos • Patricia Traxler • Christine Turner • Kathleen Tyau • Michael Upchurch • Daniel Wallace • Ed Weyhing • Joan Wickersham • Lex Williford • Gary Wilson • Terry Wolverton • Monica Wood • Christopher Woods • Celia Wren • Jane Zwinger

A Children's Party on the S.S. Manhattan, October 29th, 1934

Coming soon:

Still, the trees outside the windows grow naked every winter, each spring they bud, in summer they cast their heavy shadows. Because the seasons change around me, I think I must still be alive.

from "Cider Mill" by Wendy Counsil

Sleep is sacred business in our house. Sometimes I think her dream life, that other life of pies and ice cream, is more important than the one she lives with me.

from "Little Debbie" by Kevin Canty

Do you know the Andrew Hacker story? He wrote *Two Nations: Black and White, Separate, Hostile, Unequal.* A wonderful book. He did an experiment in the colleges where he said to young college students, "All right, everything about you stays the same, but we're going to make your skin black. What do we have to give you—in terms of money—to make this worth your while?"

Their answer was, "A million dollars for the rest of our lives."

from an interview with Toi Derricotte by Susan McInnis